Steven Truscott

and the Murder of

12-Year Old Lynne Harper

In Canada's Most Infamous Murder
127 Clues that names the Killer

Sam   Dennis
McDonough
ClueMasterSDM

Steven Truscott and the Murder of 12-year-old Lynne Harper

Copyright © 2011, Sam Dennis McDonough

Third Edition

All Rights Reserved

ISBN# 978-1-257-09455-4

This work licensed under the Creative Commons Attribution-ShareAlike 3.0 Unported License. To view a copy of this license, visit http//creativecommons.org/licenses/by-nc /2.5/, or send a letter to Creative Commons, 171 Second Street, Suite 300, San Francisco, California, 94105, USA. http//www.lulu.com

NOTE: As author and compiler, I am fully responsible for the contents in this book. "Steven Truscott and the Murder of 12-year-old-Lynne Harper" is based on facts taking from evidence obtained from public information, and in some cases sincere opinion. Feel free to disagree

Sam Dennis McDonough, Clue Master SDM

How the media or the public or the courts happen to deal with a crime has no bearing on the conclusions in my books. My passion is to **objectively search for the facts and evidence that lead to *the truth* in controversial real crimes.**

So it is with the 127 clues in this book that show who murdered little adventurous Lynne Harper. Please read this book with an open, objective, critically thinking mind. If the facts and evidence presented do not make the case for you, then continue on with whatever you believe.

Dedication

This book is dedicated to Steven Murray Truscott who very wisely said:

"I'm not asking for the world. Go over all the information. Investigate. Let the people know all the evidence, and let them judge for themselves. I'm not afraid of that. Why are they?"

September 16. 1959: Jury trial begins at Ontario Superior Court, Goderich, Tuckersmith Township, in Huron County.

Judge: *Prisoner stand-up.*
Steven Truscott's *five feet and nine inches* stands before the judge, jury and courtroom onlookers.

Jury Foreman: *We find the defendant guilty as charged with a plea for mercy.*

Judge: *Steven Murray Truscott, I have no alternative but to pass the following sentence on you. The jury has found you guilty after a fair trial. The sentence of this court upon you is that you be taken from here to the place from whence you came. And there be kept in close confinement until Tuesday, the eighth day of December, 1959. Upon that day and date you will be taken to the place of execution where you will be hanged by the neck until you are dead. May the Lord have mercy on your soul?*
Judge, looking at Steven Truscott*: Have you anything to say why the sentence of this court should not be passed upon you according to law?*

Steven Truscott: *No.*

Contents

Page

1. Chapter 1: The Disappearance of Lynne Harper
6.   Lynne Harper's Body Found in Lawson's Bush
10.   Crime Area Description
11.   Map of Crime Area

19. Chapter 2: Steven Truscott's Arrest and Trial
21.   Trial by Jury
22.   Timeline of Events
30.   Huron County Jury Decision: Guilty!
31.   Appeal Court - No New Trial for Truscott
32.   Sentence Commuted to Life

33. Chapter 3: 21 year-old Truscott Testifies at Supreme Court
35.   Timeline – Disappearance to Finding Body
47.   Truscott Denials before Supreme Court
50.   Canada Supreme Court Decision on the Appeal

55. Chapter 4: If Steven Truscott's Story were True
60.   Death Penalty for Murder Abolished in Canada

61. Chapter 5: Media Campaign to Acquit Steven Truscott

Page

63. Chapter 6: Ontario Appeal Court Reviews Conviction
68.   Truscott Acquitted by Ontario Appeal Court
72.   Compensation for Steven Truscott
73.   Steven Truscott's Ride through History

75. Chapter 7: Q and A that Show Who Killed Lynne Harper
96.   Lynne Harper's Sacrifice
96.   Facts, Logic, Critical Thinking and Justice

97. Chapter 8: Sergeant Alexander Kalichuk

99. Conclusion

103. Until Someone can Explain…

110. Space Reserved

111. Sources

About This Book

On a cold September day in 1959 a 14 year old Canadian schoolboy, in just his first encounter with the police and in a crime of passion, was sentenced by a jury to hang for the murder of his 12-year-old friend.

It is sad when any young boy is punished more harshly than should be for his crime. Fortunately, common sense prevailed and after three months the penalty was reduced to life. Six years later a journalist would write about this boy sentenced to hang until dead, always claimed he was innocent.

The truth is not for everyone, it is only for those who seek it.

Chapter 1: Lynne Harper Disappears

In the early evening of **Tuesday June 9, 1959,** 12-year-old *Cheryl* **Lynne Harper** disappeared near Royal Canadian Air Force (RCAF) Clinton, an air force base in southwestern Ontario, just south of Clinton. Before 9:00 pm, her father and brother began searching for her. At 11:20 Lynne's father reported her missing. She was last seen with Steven Truscott.

Steven *Murray* Truscott (born January 18, 1945) was a 14 ½ year old boy in the same classroom as Lynne at A.V.M. Hugh Campbell School on the air force base. Steven was in the 8th grade in their combined classroom and Lynne was in the 7th.

6:15 pm: After dinner, wearing only turquoise shorts, a white sleeveless blouse and brown loafers, Lynne walked to the schoolyard and cheerfully helped **Mrs. Nickerson** with the Junior Girl Guides. Mrs. Nickerson said she saw Steven cycling down a pathway towards them shortly before **7:00** and stop nearby. Lynne went to him and sat on his bicycle wheel. Truscott acknowledged being with Lynne the evening she was killed. He was seen with her on his bicycle after **7:00 pm** in close proximity to Lawson's Bush, a 20 acre woodlot. *(Clue 1)*

7:10-7:15: We know for a fact that Steven and Lynne did push his bike onto County Road where Lynne sat on the crossbar. We also know for a fact that the two proceeded northbound down the road towards the Bayfield Bridge and we can follow Steven and Lynne on the bike until they reach Lawson's bush to their right without hearing a single dissenting voice.

Upon Truscott's return to the school yard just after **8:00 pm,** there was curiosity among his classmates about what had happened to Lynne and a rumor was buzzing amongst some kids that something bad had happened in Lawson's Bush.

Several children had seen Steven leave with her; he came back alone. *(Clue 2)*

Mr. Harper reported Lynne missing at **11:20 pm.**

June 10, 1959, Morning
At first light RCAF Officer Lesley Harper, frantic with worry, went house to house on the base, desperate for news of his missing daughter. He got a lead when someone reported seeing Lynne near the schoolyard the previous evening around 7:10 pm. She was perched on the crossbar of classmate Steven Truscott's green racing bicycle as the husky fourteen-year-old pedaled toward County Road, which ran north of the air base.

Flying Officer **Mr. Harper** rushed to the Truscott residence for information about his daughter. He told **Mrs. Truscott** that Lynne was missing and he heard that Steven was the last person to see her. Mrs. Truscott called Steven to the door where Mr. Harper asked Steven if had seen Lynne. Young Steven told him that he had given Lynne a ride to Highway 8 because she'd wanted to see some ponies at a house nearby. **He could not recall anything else said during that meeting.** Air Force Officer Harper said he felt that "**Truscott had his answer ready**". *(Clue 3)*

Later that morning, Constable **Donald Hobbs** had the following conversation with Truscott:

Hobbs: Steven, do you know that Lynne Harper is missing?
Steven: Yes

Hobbs: Did you give Lynne a ride on a motorcycle?
Steven: I gave her a ride on a bicycle, not a motorcycle.

Hobbs: Where did you pick Lynne up?
Steven: Outside the school.

Hobbs: What time was it?
Steven: At about 7:25 and 7:30

Hobbs: Did she say anything to you?
Steven: She said she knew the people in the little white house along the highway and might go down to see the ponies. She said she had to be home by 8:00 or 8:30.

Hobbs: Where did you drop her off?
Steven: I took her to the highway and dropped her off, and then I returned to the bridge over the river.

Hobbs: Did you see Lynne again?
Steven: Yes, I did. I looked back and saw her get into a car. I believe it to be a late model grey Chevy with a lot of chrome and it could have been a Bel Air. The car appeared to have a yellow licence plate. There was no one in the rear; I am not sure how many were in the front.

The officers stirred. This was promising. Each year thousands of tourists from Michigan, just an hour's drive to the southwest, cross the border into Ontario. The bright yellow Michigan plates were easy to spot.

Truscott said he met Lynne at the Brownies and that she was in a chatty, happy mood. He said she asked for a ride to Highway 8 so she could see ponies at a white house just east of County Road. He stated that we pushed the bike between us across the school yard. I got on the seat, she mounted the crossbar and we took off. *(5)* Steven said he passed **Richard Gellanty prior to reaching the bush tractor trail** and that he took Lynne past the bush and over the bridge where he waved to **Arnold (Butch) George, Douglas Oaks** and **Jerry Durnin**. *(Clue 4)* Steven said he continued to Highway 8 where he left Lynne unharmed, saying she would hitch the rest of the way.

Steven said that, as he cycled back, he stopped on the bridge overlooking the Bayfield River and a popular swimming hole. He happened to glance back just in time to see **Lynne's arm up hitchhiking and then climb into the front seat of a 1959 gray Bel Air Chevy,** which sped off east along Highway 8. Steven said the time was about 7:30 pm. *(1, 16)*

Truscott said, "*From the bridge I watched Doug Oaks at the swimming hole for five or ten minutes and I waved at Butch George a school chum.* (5) *(Clue 5)* Then I went to the schoolyard where I chatted with my brother and friends." (*1, 5, 10*) When police asked him if anyone made a comment to him after he returned to the schoolyard he replied: "I believe one asked me, **'What did you do with Harper, feed her to the fish?' I said I took her and let her off at Highway 8.**"

June 10, Wednesday: Truscott told F/Sgt. Johnson and Sergeant Anderson of the Ontario Provincial Police (OPP) that he and Lynne met Richard Gellatly a short distance south of the tractor trail. Gellatly had told the police he was riding south on the county road to get swimming trunks from home **when he met Steven and Lynne between the school and Lawson's Bush**. That was about **7:15-7:20** on June 9th, the last time anyone, other than Truscott, was known to see Lynne alive. When he returned 10 minutes later he did not see either. *(Clue 6)*

Later that day, Truscott told police that he looked at the school clock which showed 7:30 as he and Lynne left the school. *(Clue 7)*

June 10, Wednesday Evening: Boys are playing around at a bridge when this conversation takes place:

Paul Desjardine: Steve, did you take Lynne into the woods?
Steven: I didn't.

Paul: Arnold said you did.
Steven: Butch, did you say I took Lynne Harper in the woods?
Butch: No

What happened the next afternoon was highly significant. After at least five interviews with Steven, investigators made an order for the next day to have a 250-man search team to fan out, not along Highway 8 where Steven claimed he had last seen Lynne, but on County Road itself.

The county road where Steven and Lynne rode double on his bike and the bush area where the body of Lynne Harper was found

June 11 -- Thursday Morning: Butch George confirmed to the police that he saw Steven pass over the bridge alone on June 9th. *(5)*

OPP Constable Donald **Hobbs:** Is there anything else you remembered regarding Lynne?
Steven Truscott: one thing. She had a gold chain necklace. It was a heart with the RCAF crest on it. *(Clue 8)*

This was the first time anyone had mentioned Lynne's locket. Police then repeated questions that Steven had answered.

Hobbs: While you were cycling, did you see anyone else?
Steven: I passed Richard Gellatly on the road and then at the river I spotted Butch George and waved to him. *(Clue 9)*

Hobbs: About what time was it when you left with Lynne?
Steven: Seven o'clock or shortly after. *(Clue 10)*

Lynne Harper's Body Found

1959, June 11, Thursday: Mostly the road cut through open wheat fields, but about three-quarters of a mile north of the air base, on the eastern side of the road, lay a 20 acre wooded area known locally as Lawson's Bush. Trooping down a tractor trail and across a barbed-wire fence, the searchers entered a tangle of elm, ash, and maple. About 2:00 pm, in a scrub-filled hollow less than 100 feet from the paved road, the search for Lynne ended.

Two days after Lynne disappeared, RCAF searchers found her partially nude body. Someone had strangled her by winding and knotting her sleeveless blouse tightly around her neck.

There is no doubt about the place of death: the position of the body, the scuff marks, a footprint at her feet, and the flattening of the vegetation between her legs, indicated rape, or attempted rape, had taken place. However, the leaves around her body were undisturbed, with *no piles of dirt, scraped earth, or broken branches to suggest a violent struggle.*

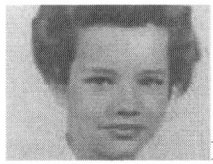Lynne Harper's life cut short at just 12 years.

Removing Lynne's body

Lynne was lying on her back, naked except for her underskirt and blouse, which had been torn and knotted tightly around her neck. *Most of her clothing was removed and piled up near where the body lay. Her brown loafers were placed side by side, her turquoise shorts zipped up, and her socks neatly rolled. Her panties were found 33 feet away. The eerie neatness of the crime scene, with its carefully laid-out clothes, and little bruising on the body*, **suggest some degree of compliance.** (10, p. 9) Police found bike tire tracks nearby.

The wounds were consistent with having been made by twigs scattered around the ground. There were several puncture wounds on her back and shoulders and a small quantity of blood on the dandelion leaves at the fork of her body. Under her left shoulder police found a red button that appeared to have been ripped from her blouse when forming the ligature used to strangle her. *The button shows that the girl was killed where she lay and was not carried there.* Three branches from an ash tree lay across her body are the only signs that the killer was in panic.

That afternoon Dr. John Penistan, a pathologist with the Attorney General of Ontario, studied the body. With temperatures staying around 90 degrees for the past few days, decomposition was well advanced. Lynne had been strangled, and he suspected that rape had at least been attempted, if not completed. Dr. Penistan spotted two small mounds of earth in the ground between Lynne's ankles, likely formed by the rapist's shoes as he struggled to accomplish intercourse. After concluding his preliminary examination, the body was turned on its left side so that the ground beneath could be photographed.

Together with **Dr. David Hall Brooks**, chief medical officer at the air base, **Dr Penistan** performed the autopsy on Lynne Harper's body. **The local coroner put Lynne Harper's time of death as prior to 7:45 p.m. on June 9. He based this opinion on the degree of decomposition of her body, the extent to which the body was still affected by rigor mortis, and the state of the contents of Lynne's stomach.**

The answer lay in the stomach. Her mother said that Lynne last at 5:30 pm. Eager to be out in the summer sunshine, she downed a meal of turkey, cranberry sauce, peas, and potatoes, finishing with a slice of upside-down pineapple cake for dessert, before leaving the house no later than 5:45 pm. About one pound of easily recognizable remains of the meal was still in Lynne's stomach. Dr. Penistan felt certain that a healthy girl like Lynne was killed soon after eating, allowing for considerable volume and only partial digestion of the food in her stomach.

Moving Lynne Harper's body from Lawson's Bush

Dr. Penistan also said that the attempt, or the act of intercourse, had taken place "while the child was dying, when the heart stopped or had almost stopped beating." He concluded that although injuries to the body were severe, there was little bleeding from them. (5)

June 11, Thursday

OPP called in **Harold Graham** of the Criminal Investigations Branch (**CIB**). Truscott was not a strong suspect at this time.

8

Police activity near Lawson's Bush on June 11, 1959

Friday, June 12

Ontario Attorney General Kelso Roberts put up the highest bounty ever for her killer, **$10,000 "dead or alive"**.

10:45 am: Inspector Graham wanted a detailed account from Steven because he was the last person known to have seen Lynne alive. **Steven gave Graham** new details about seeing Lynne.   **Steven:** She had her thumb out. A car swerved in off the edge of the road and pulled out. She got in the front seat and the car pulled away going east toward Seaforth. After returning from the highway I lingered at the bridge for "about five minutes" and on my way back "I waved at Arnold George at the river." **Steven** also said he saw four boys at the river: Butch, Dougie Oates, Gerry Durnin and Gary Gilks.

Graham: Are you interested in girls?
Steven: Some

Graham: Were you ever out with Lynne Harper?
Steven: No, no one was interested in her...none of them liked her much. Sort of bossy in school...she didn't appeal to boys.

Steven also told Graham that he had heard that an adult named Audrey Jackson had spotted Lynne on the base Tuesday evening around 8:30 pm. (Actually, she had seen her about 6:30 pm.)

Crime Area Description

On the next page is a sketch map to help understand the crime area and the evidence as it was in 1959.

The RCAF Station is at the southerly end of a county road which goes north to King's Highway No. 8 which runs east and west.

On leaving the station immediately to the right is the Bob Lawson farm. The 20 acres of second growth ash, elm and maple referred to as "Lawson's bush" or "the bush" or "the woods", and is the specific section of bush just east of County Road at the tractor trail entrance. *(5)*

Distance from the southerly end of the county road to the tractor trail is **3,366 feet** (2/3 mile).

Distance from the tractor trail north to the Canadian National Railway crossing is **1,568 feet** (1/3 mile).

Distance from railroad crossing north to the road bridge is **491 ft**.

Distance from the Bayfield River Bridge north to the intersection of County Road and Highway 8 is **1300 feet** (1/4 mile).
Visible from the bridge about **642** feet east is a swimming hole where the kids hang out.

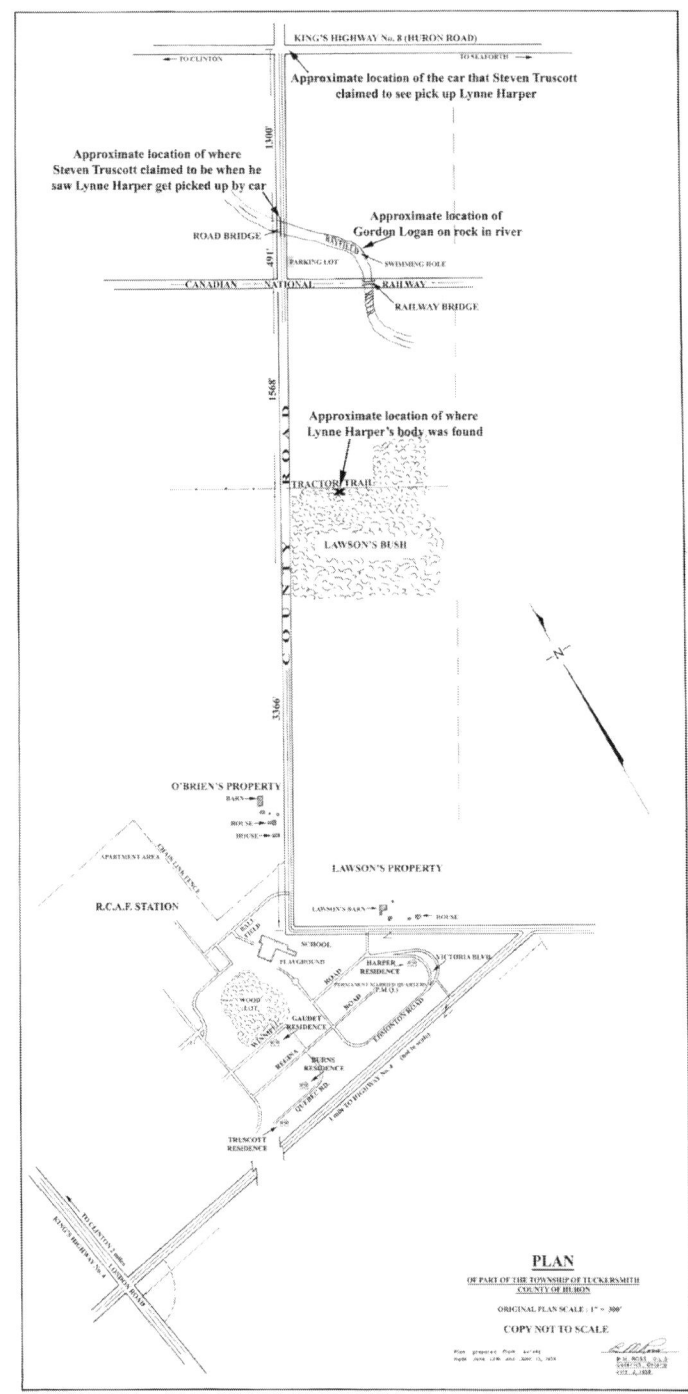

APPENDIX 1 - MAP OF THE COUNTY ROAD AND SURROUNDING AREA

Arial view of County Road and Lawson's Bush

June 12:

The regional pathologist said that most of Lynne's last meal was still in her stomach and in the early phase of digestion. Lynne's stomach consisted of about one pint of poorly masticated, slightly digested food, including peas, potatoes, and some meat

All the while, Lynne's stomach contents are in the early natural phases of digestion. We know for a fact that Lynne Harper had only recently finished her dinner, we know that her system was in the early stages of digestion – and we know that the process of digestion stops at death. These are simple facts, and they are as true today as they were in 1959. Lynne's parents said she ate at 5:30-5:45. *(5)* *(15, p. 330)*

Dr. J. A. Addison examined Steven and found a cut on his leg, scratches on his torso and on each side of his penis, "a brush burn of two or three day's duration the size of a 25-cent piece." They were located just behind the groove on the lateral side of the penis. Steven's penis appeared swollen and slightly reddened on the distal end…by stretching the skin and pulling it upwards towards the body, there were two raw sores with serum oozing from them. Addison's findings were confirmed by Dr. Brooks. *(Clue 11)*

Steven Truscott's story was beginning to look unbelievable.

In the cellar of Steven's home, searchers found the **red jeans** he had been wearing on the night in question, **freshly laundered and hanging alone on a line.** Despite being washed, faint traces of grass stains were discernible on the knees and on one leg there was a tear that corresponded with the injury on Steven's leg.

Police found that the Steven's bicycle tire tread pattern was identical to that found at the crime scene.

The circumstantial evidence was now piling up. So far as the police were concerned, there had been no gray Chevrolet, no yellow license plate, and no stranger stopping to give Lynne Harper a ride. It had all been the cunning fabrication of a brutal killer desperate to cover his tracks. The way they figure it, Steve had lured Lynne into Lawson's Bush with the intention of having intercourse; then, when she resisted, he had raped and strangled her. Disregard the suspect's age, they reasoned, and this case was just one more squalid sex murder, the kind of tragedy repeated countless times across Canada every year.

Although the police were convinced they had their killer they still didn't have a full proof case. When they attempted to re-create the final few minutes of Lynne Harper's brief life, holes began to appear in the timeline, primarily because all major eyewitnesses to the tragic events of June 9 were young children, none of whom had a time piece. Therefore the stories they told were so contradictory, so perverse, as to confound reasoned analysis.

Until someone can explain why anyone would believe Steven's story that Lynne wanted to go 1.2 miles to the highway to **hitch-hike alone at 7:30 if she had to be home by 8:30 pm.** *(Clue 12)*

Until someone explains why the *Fifth Estate's* biased movie showed Lynne on the ***handle bars*** instead of the crossbar as was told by Steven and every witness who saw them? *(Clue 13)*

Until someone can explain why generous good-hearted Steven Truscott, after taking Lynne 1.2 miles to the highway, *would not offer to take her .3 miles further to the pony farm?*

Until someone explains why anyone would believe that a decent boy would take a petite 12-year-old girl friend on his bicycle crossbar and *then leave her alone at an isolated intersection one hour before dark*.

Until someone explains why they accept *Steven's story that Lynne wanted a ride to the highway to see ponies* and when she got there decided to hitch-hike to who knows where? *(Clue 14)*

Until someone can explain the above five evidences of guilt, I will have full confidence that Steven Truscott murdered petite Lynne Harper in Lawson's Bush.

Until someone can explain why they believe Truscott's story of hitch-hiking when there is *absolutely no evidence that Lynne was planning to leave her home and her parents* and head east with the first stranger who would pick her up.

Until someone comes forward with evidence that Lynne had the *desire* or *disposition to run away from home, I will be confident that Truscott murdered Lynne Harper in Lawson's Bush.*

Until someone can explain why they accept Truscott's kindness for taking Lynne to the highway, *but forgive him for leaving his friend alone and not conversing with her.* Steven always said that he just took her there, let her off, and rode back to the bridge.

Until Truscott explains why after seeing his girl friend suddenly in danger, doesn't mention this tragic event to his friends at the bridge. If this story were true, even Truscott would have the maturity and decency *to tell someone; perhaps the girl's father.* *(Clue 15)*

Until someone can explain why Steven *Truscott did not tell school chums or his brother* that he had given Lynne Harper a ride to the intersection where he saw her get into a stranger's 1959 Chevy Bel Air car; and speed off with her and that she is probably in danger for her life. *The time to say this was after he was asked if he threw Lynne Harper to the fish.* (Clue 16)

Until someone can explain the above five evidence of guilt, I will have full confidence that Steven Truscott murdered Lynne Harper in Lawson's Bush.

Until Steven Truscott can tell us why he did not notify anyone that he saw his girl friend hitch a ride with a stranger, I will be confident that Steven Truscott killed Lynne Harper. 6 (*Clue 17*)

Until someone can explain why Truscott supporters believe, without question, his wild unbelievable story that a mysterious stranger picked Lynne up on the highway, rode around with her for hours without feeding her, would reverse his direction *and return her, not to the intersection where he picked her up, but to kill her in Truscott's favorite place in a dark 20 acre bush;* all without leaving one piece of evidence that he was there. *(Clue 18)*

Until someone can explain why, after a sleepless grief-stricken night, Lynne's father *had to go to Steven Truscott at his home to find out what he did with his 12-year-od daughter*. *(Clue 19)*

Until Steven Truscott tells us why he told Mr. Harper only that Lynne *wanted a ride to see some ponies and that he rode her to the Highway 8 where he left her unharmed*. *(Clue 20)*

Until Steven Truscott tells *us why he did not tell the concerned father* that he was sorry he had left his 12-year-old daughter alone at the intersection one hour before dark.

Until someone can explain the above five evidences of guilt, I will have full confidence that Steven Truscott murdered Lynne Harper in Lawson's Bush.

Until Truscott tells us why he did not tell the worried father his favorite story *that he saw her hitch-hiking to who knows where.* He saves that story for his first police interview. *(Clue 21)*

Until Truscott tells us why he did not tell the grieving father that *he saw Lynne get into a stranger's 1959 Chevrolet Bel Air and that he saw the car speeding east down highway 8.* *(Clue 22)*

Until Truscott tells why he would tell his unbelievable story to the police later that morning, *but not earlier to Lynne's father?*

Until someone can explain the odds *that a driver or passenger on this busy highway would not see a girl, or boy, or girl and boy* during the 10 minutes Truscott says they were there. *(Clue 23)*

Until someone can explain why anyone would believe the made up story that the only car to stop for Lynne would happen to be *a stranger who would harm her?*

Until someone can explain the above five evidences of guilt, I will have full confidence that Steven Truscott murdered Lynne Harper in Lawson's Bush.

Until someone explains why Truscott's supporters believe, against all odds, *that he would also happen to be a pedophile?*

Until someone explains how this brainless pedophile *would, in the dark, happen to pick the same woodlot that Truscott said he and Lynne rode by just a few hours earlier.* *(Clue 24)*

June 12, 1959

Until Steven Truscott has a *believable reason why he had two raw lesions* the size of quarters on either side of his penis shaft *just days after he was the last person seen with Lynne Harper before she was raped and murdered.*

Until Steven Truscott tells us that he really did tell the truth to three different police officers on three different occasions that he and Richard Gallantry passed each other before reaching the bush and that he later lied under oath that he did not see Gallantry. Truscott also lied to the Supreme Court Justices that he never told any police officer that he saw or passed Gellatlty.

Until Steven Truscott tells us why: when friends teased him about being in the woods with Lynne, *he told them a story about looking for calves in the bush.* When police questioned him, *he invented a new Chevrolet at the highway.* When his penis sores were found *his stories changed with every telling.* *(Clue 25)*

Until someone can explain the above five evidences of guilt, I will have full confidence that Steven Truscott murdered Lynne Harper in Lawson's Bush and has spent the rest of his life fooling with the Canadian people and their tax money.

Until someone can explain why so many people believe that every adult and kid in this story is a liar except Truscott.

OPP Inspector Graham and his officers interviewed over a dozen students on Friday and he heard *Jocelyne's account of a secret meeting* with Steven. In addition, the Attorney General's Laboratory sent information on *Lynne's stomach contents* that showed her last meal was ingested less than two hours prior to her death.

June 12, 1959, 6:50 pm: *Less than 24 hours after arriving on the scene Inspector Graham* decides that Steven Truscott needs to be brought in to sign or change his statements or even confess because of the following evidences. *Clue 26)*

Jocelyne's account about a meeting with Steven near the bush **Steven was the last person known to see Lynne Harper alive.** He was last seen with Lynne near where her body was found. **In test, Truscott could not see from the bridge things and events that he claimed to have seen.**
Laboratory results of Lynne's stomach contents show that she died within two hours after eating.
Two doctors report the penis sores

After one more interview **the police were convinced that Steven took Lynne Harper into Lawson's Bush where her body was found,** and that no one picked Lynne up on the highway, rode around for hours, returned to the area from which he picked her up, not to let her off at the intersection, but to take her into the dark woods to kill her in Lawson's Bush. *(Clue 27)*

Police began to sense that Steven had schemed to lure a girl – any girl – to Lawson's Bush, with the intention of having intercourse. After Jocelyne postponed their meeting, he'd gone hunting for another girl and found Lynne Harper. Once in the bush, she had tried to fight off his advances, but the muscular 14 year old, hormones throbbing in a sexual frenzy, strangled her.

Truscott's unbelievable tale of Lynne hitching a ride with a stranger and being brought back to his favorite place in the bush was enough to call him in. The 5'9" 131 lb boy had committed a man's murder and needed to pay for his crime. About 7:00 pm Truscott was taken into custody. His underpants, taken off at the jail, were fouled and soiled. They showed male sperm and minute quantities of blood, particularly around the zipper. *(Clue 28)*

Chapter 2: Truscott's Arrest and Trial

1959

June 13, *Saturday about 2:30 am:* Steven Truscott was charged with first degree murder under provisions of the Juvenile Delinquents Act.

June 15: After numerous amendments, Butch George ruefully admitted that he had lied to help a friend; that on the evening of June 10th, Steven had asked him to tell police that he saw Steven when he crossed over the bridge with Lynne. Butch George agreed to tell the police that he saw Steven down at the river. After her body was found he decided to tell the truth.

June 19: Ten year old Sandra Archibald finds a heart-shaped chain necklace hanging on a wire fence near County Road. The locket was in the grass and the heart was outside the fence.

Even after Steven's arrest, new witnesses continued to come forward. Allan Oats, older brother of Douglas, claimed that he, too, had been on County Road that night, close to Lawson's Bush, and had spotted Steven standing alone on the bridge. All of these sightings paled, reckoned the police, when set against the evidence of Arnold George. Although this 13-year olds various statements were patchy and inconsistent, the final version he settled upon painted Steven in the worse light imaginable.

During Steven's first police interview – before the body had been found – he mentioned waving to Arnold George near the river at the crucial time. Subsequently, Arnold confirmed that Steven passed over the bridge alone; however, after numerous amendments, he admitted that he had lied to help a friend.

June 20: Steven Truscott's appeal is dismissed. He is ordered to be tried as an adult.

July 12: In mid-July Juvenile Court Judge Dudley Holmes presided over a preliminary hearing to determine if there was sufficient evidence to proceed with an actual trial.

The case against Steven Truscott was that he met Lynne Harper on the school grounds of the Clinton RCAF. Station at about 7.00 on the evening of June 9, 1959, and that at about 7:15 they were seen riding north on County Road with her on his bicycle crossbar. They met **Richard Gellatly south of Lawson's Bush. Various witnesses on the County Road testified that they did not see Truscott or Lynne north of Lawson's Bush and at least two witnesses were actively looking for them. The police believed that about half way between the school and Highway 8, Truscott turned into the bush and killed Lynne. Her body was found in the bush two days later.**

Among other witnesses during the Preliminary Hearing:

Defense Counsel Donnelly questioned Butch George.

Donnelly: During the time you were swimming did you see Steven Truscott?
George: No

Donnelly: So you saw him at no time after you left the station at about 7:00 until you returned home about 8:30?
George: That is right.

Donnelly: Did you see Steven go into the woods with Lynne?
George: No

Toward the end **Magistrate Holmes turned to Truscott:** Having heard the evidence, do you wish to say anything in answer to the charge?

Donnelly: the accused does not wish to make a statement.

July 14: After hearing 31 witnesses and examining 21 pieces of evidence in two days, Magistrate Holmes declared, "the evidence is sufficient to put the accused on trial.

Trial by Jury

September 16. 1959: Jury trial begins at the Ontario Superior Court, Goderich, Tuckersmith Township, in Huron County.

The Crown's case was primarily circumstantial since it relied on this evidence: **1) Steven was the last person to see Lynne alive. 2) His statements contain inconsistencies. 3) He asked a witness to corroborate, falsely, what he had told the police. 4) Time of death fell within the time Steven was with Lynne. 5) Talk that Steven intended to have sexual relations that evening. 6.) SuspiciousPenis lesions.** *(Clue 30)*

On the defense version of the County Road evidence, Truscott said that Lynne asked him to give her a ride on his bicycle to the intersection of the county road and Highway 8. He let her off and headed back southbound on County Road. He last saw Lynne a few minutes after he dropped her off when he looked back from the bridge and saw her getting into a new Chevrolet driven by an unknown man that sped off east towards Seaforth.

The Crown maintained that it was physically impossible for Truscott to see from 1300 feet what he claimed to have seen and that he deliberately fabricated the story to mislead police about what had happened to Lynne Harper. *(15, p. 570) Clue 31*

Even before this, police officers had been deeply suspicious of Steven's manner and particularly his claim that he saw Lynne being picked up by someone in a '59 Chevy on Highway 8, while he stood on the bridge, 1300 feet away. The police doubted that anyone could identify a car at that distance, even being able to pick out the color of its license plates.

Constable **Trumbley** testified that when he and Steven returned to the police car where his mother was seated, Constable Trumbley told her that Steven "couldn't see any license plates at all", to which Mrs. Truscott responded, "Maybe it was one of those yellow signs like we have on our car from Fairyland Gardens."*(15, p. 570) Clue 32*

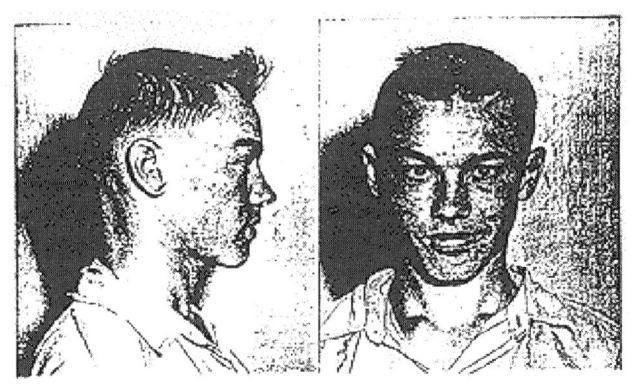

TRUSCOTT Steven Murray
Age 14 yrs.
Height 5ft. 8½ in.
Weight 131 lbs.

Timeline of Events

(Dates are accurate but times could be several minutes either side of the printed time because the events were not important at the time and no child had a time piece.)

Tuesday, June 9, 1959: Jocelyne Goddette (13) testified that Steven arranged to meet her to see two new calves. *They were to meet just outside the fence by Lawson's Bush at 6:00 pm and she was not to tell or bring anyone. She said Steven came to her house about 5:50, but they were eating so she told him she would meet him later.* (15, p. 386) Clue 33

Since noon on that very hot day, kids from the base had either cycled or walked up County Road to cool off in the swimming hole, which was situated on the Bayfield River, about halfway between Lawson's Bush and Highway 8.

Tuesday, June 9, 1959:

6:20 pm: After dinner, wearing only turquoise shorts, a white sleeveless blouse and brown loafers, **Lynne Harper** walked to the school grounds where she cheerfully helped **Mrs. Nickerson** with the Junior Guides.

6:30 pm: Truscott told the police that after he left home on his bicycle he went first to the school grounds. Finding no one there he rode to the river. (6:35 pm). He saw no one at the river so he turned around a couple of times and went back to the station. (6:55 pm) *Truscott maintains that he met no one on the way down or back.*

Paul Desjardine (14*), rode north on his bicycle to go fishing at Bayfield Bridge. He testified that he met Steven a short distance south of Lawson's bush.* They said nothing to each other. Steven was alone and was riding his bicycle around in circles on the county road.

6:35 pm: Mrs. Beatrice Geiger *(32) was riding a bicycle to the bridge when she passed Steven at the bush area riding his bicycle. They were both going north.* Steven went as far as the bridge, stopped a second or two, took a look around and headed south again. She met him the second time at about the railroad tracks. *(5)* **Ronald Demaray** (17) saw Steven on his green bike on the bridge and said that he seemed to be just looking around.

6:40 pm: Kenneth Geiger (12) and **Robb Harrington** were riding double on their way to the river when they saw Truscott sitting on his bicycle in the middle of the road opposite the "tractor trail." He was looking towards the station. Kenneth told the police that *Steven said, "Mrs. Geiger was at the bridge" and Kenneth said he knew that. Then both continued on their way.*

6:50 pm: Jocelyne leaves home **to *go to the bush for her meeting with Steven;*** not finding him there she cycles to Steve's friend, Bob Lawson at his barn **(7:15).** She tells Bob she is looking for Steven. She leaves at **7:25** to return to the bush.

6:55 – 7:05 pm: *Mrs. Nickerson said that Steven came cycling on the pathway towards them around 7:00 pm and stopped nearby. Lynne went over to talk to Steven.* *(5)*

Truscott said he rode back to the schoolyard and was watching the Brownies when Lynne came over and sat on the front fender of his bicycle. He remembers little of what they talked about.

Truscott did remember that Lynne asked him for a ride to No. 8 Highway. After a few minutes, "we pushed the bike together to the county road, she got on the crossbar and we took off." *(5)*

7:15 pm: Steven and Lynne's leave the schoolyard, with fixed reasonable certainty by the evidence of Mrs. Nickerson and Mrs. Bohonus at *7:10, no later than 7:15 pm.* *(5)*

7:15pm: Farmer Lawson said Jocelyne was at his barn and told him she was looking for Steven. She left about ten minutes later to look again for Steven at their arranged meeting place outside of Lawson's Bush. *(Clue 34)*

7:15: Meanwhile, one mile north two boys left the swimming hole and headed south on the same road. One, Richard Gellatly (12) was cycling south on County Road to get his swimming suit from home **when he met Steven and Lynne on County Road between the school and the bush. Truscott confirmed their meeting to three different officers.** The other boy, Philip Burns (10) was on foot. Since the only intersection on County Road between the swimming hole and the school grounds was railroad tracts, any road users heading in opposite directions would pass within a few feet of each other.

Tuesday, June 9, 1959

7:20: And so it proved. **Richard on his bike met and passed Steven and Lynne just south of Lawson's Bush.** Thinking no more of it Richard cycled on.

7:30: Five or ten minutes later, **a walking Philip reached the Bush. He told police that he did not see Steven or Lynne on County Road.** If true, this meant that shortly after they met Richard that Steven with Lynne on his crossbar had turned off of County Road and into Lawson's Bush. *5;* (10 p. 257-8) *Clue 35*

One person that Philip Burns *did* meet on County Road that evening was Jocelyne Goddette (13). Burns was alongside Lawson's Bush when Jocelyne came breathlessly cycling toward him, asking if he had seen Steven. When he said no, Jocelyne frowned with disappointment.

Jocelyne had returned to Lawson's Bush and was looking for Steven or Lynne when Butch George rode up. (She later told the police and testified in court that Steve was to show her a calf in Lawson's Bush that evening, but a late supper had forced her to say no.) *Soon all three were looking for Steven or Lynne around the bush area where they were last seen. The three searchers fail to find a sign of either.* (At about that same time Steven said that he and Lynne were cycling past the river.)

7:45: Jocelyne checked one more time at the swimming hole but he was not there either. Disappointed she abandoned her search and for the final time that evening she cycled slowly past the bush right past the body of Lynne Harper about 80 feet in from the road. She shouted Steven's name. She received no answer.

8:00: Jocelyne checked in once more with Bob Lawson for a few minutes and then arrived home before 8:30.

8:00-8:10: Steven Truscott returns to the school grounds looking his normal self: relaxed, calm and collected.

June 9 - 11:20 pm: Lynne's father reports her missing to Air Force police.

Truscott told the police that he did not see Jocelyne, Philip Burns, Bryan Glover, Tom Gillette or others. The fact is that Steven would have passed right by them on this straight road if he had continued on to the Highway 8.

Steven tells us that no stop was made at the tractor trail and no stop made at Lawson's bush. If true, it took them less than a minute to approach the trail from the road and then pass it by.

Steven tells us they continued their journey down the road to the highway. He tells us that Lynne's plan was to see ponies at a little white house just east along the highway before returning home before dark, in less than one hour. (10, p. 50).

Meanwhile, further north two youngsters at the swimming hole, Gordon Logan and Douglas Oats, claim to have seen Steven and Lynne heading north across the river bridge.

There is no suggestion anywhere that Lynne would have to hitchhike the short distance to the pony farm. (10, p. 50) Steven tells us that Lynne was mad at her mother about not going swimming and that she may go to her grandmother 80 miles away. But she doesn't tell him she intended to run away from home and her parents on this school night by hitching a ride.

June 11: Bob Lawson, a close friend of Truscott tells police that about 10 on the night Lynne went missing he saw a convertible parked near where Lynne's body was found. It was very dark but he saw a man and maybe a girl inside.

The defense called three witnesses, Gordon "Gord" Logan (13), Douglas Oates (12) and Alan Oates (16), who lent support to Truscott's statement that he had given Lynne a ride on County Road across the bridge and that he had returned to the bridge a few minutes later alone. *(5)*

Gord insists that as he looked up from fishing in the river he saw Steven and Lynne as they crossed the bridge. *He saw them from a distance of more than two football fields and looking into a setting western sun,* (10, p. 235) *(Clue 36)* Douglas Oats says he was standing on the bridge when Steven and Lynne rode past. Strong as Douglas Oates statement is, does it make sense when applied to Truscott's version of events? *Is Steven's own story believable enough to stand on its own without Douglas Oats story?* **Does Steven's unbelievable story destroy the case against him?** *(14, 15, p. 324))* *(Clue 36)*

Until someone can explain why Jocelyne would be looking for Steven Truscott on the right hand side of the county road *if he had not previously told her to meet him there? (Clue 37)*

Until someone explains why Truscott asked a girl friend into the woods to see calves rather than a boy or his friend Butch George?

Until someone can explain why Steven Truscott proposed a secret date with Jocelyne Goddette to see calves in the woods and *told her not to tell anybody and not to bring anyone? (Clue 38)*

Until someone can explain the above three evidences of guilt, I will have full confidence that Steven Truscott murdered Lynne Harper in Lawson's Bush.

To this day, Truscott denies ever inviting Jocelyne into Lawson's bush. So which of the two stories has the ring of truth? Now, if Jocelyne had a beef with Steven, she sure found an ugly way to get even. What could Steven have done to anger Jocelyne to this extreme? Did he break a movie date with her, or sneak a kiss on the sly with her best friend? Whatever, Jocelyne never took any teenage revenge like telling him off in their classroom or in front of the gang at the Custard Cup. **This kid would get her revenge on the witness stand at Truscott's murder trial by telling a deliberate lie that would send him to his death?** *(14)* Clue 39

Until You Are Dead paints Jocelyne as a liar ("a girl few of her classmates or teachers trusted" (10, p. 125), but ***never once does it explain away the fact of her being at the bush on Tuesday just yards away from where the body is found on Thursday.*** If she lies about a planned meeting with Steven and knows nothing about the whereabouts of Lynne , then why does she look for Steven at the bush (evidence of Lawson) and then look for Steve and Lynne at the same place (evidence of Burns)? *(14) Clue 40*

Jocelyne is obviously there for a reason. *(14)* No one knows for certain how Lynne got into the bush area. Mr. Bowman for the Crown submitted that Truscott may have taken Lynne in through the section of fence where her locket was found. *(15)*

Truscott and his supporters say Butch George is a liar. First he tells the police that he waved to Steven at the bridge. Then, after Lynne's body is found he says he never saw Steven on County Road. If he did not see him, then he did not see Steven take Lynne into the bush. We know that George and Jocelyne were looking for Steven and Lynne at the bush and did not seriously search elsewhere, not at the bridge or at the highway. *(14) Clue 41*

Assume Butch George is a liar. Assume he has no reason to put Steven or Lynne in the bush, and no reason to pick the bush as the place for his lies. He could have put them together at the Custard Cup or at someone's barn. However, ***he selects the bush for his lie, the same place where Jocelyne looks for Steven and/or Lynne*** (evidence Lawson, Burns*) and the same place where Butch joins in the search* (evidence Burns).*Clue 42*

The credibility of George is not the point. Like Jocelyne, he is there looking for Steven and Lynne where Lynne's body will be found – the bush. If Harper was never there then there was no reason to look for her there, then we have a pointless search by these two kids, followed by the impossible coincidence **that she is there** *and she was strangled to death.* Clue 43

Truscott would have us believe that a few minutes after leaving Lynne she would stick her thumb out and without hesitation jump in a car with a complete stranger. (*Clue 44*)

Some of the talk was about Lynne wanting to go the pony place. So why did he let her off at the intersection instead of taking her to the pony farm? How was she supposed to get home? What's she doing getting into a strange car, and at such a late hour? **Most residents were beginning to think that a lot of things about Truscott's story didn't make any sense.**

Then whoever picked her up would have had to bring her back to Lawson's bush, dead or alive, unnoticed by any of the people out looking for her. *This story is crucial to Truscott's claims of innocence, yet the more you think about the story the more you have to shake your head in disbelief.* **Steven's story in nearly every detail lacks the ring of truth.** *(14)Clue 45*

The defense theory is that someone attacked Harper elsewhere and brought her back to the bush, but this is contrary to medical evidence which shows that she bled where her body was found. In addition, one of her buttons was found under her body. *(Clue 46)* The defense claims that Truscott had little time to kill Lynne and return to his mates with few signs of struggle. Common sense tells us that, **unless he is a psychopath,** there would be more signs that he had just killed a girl. *(Clue 47)*

The Case went to the jury with five witnesses saying they did not see Steven or Lynne on County Road, and **two were actively looking for them.** The problem for the jurors in this mostly circumstantial case is that they must use critical thinking to determine the truth. *They must actually think for them-selves and consider what they saw and heard from witness testimony.*

In charging the jury the trial judge had two undisputed facts from which to start. Firstly, that her dead body was found in Lawson's bush so someone had brought her there, alive or dead. The charge is that Truscott had taken Lynne into Lawson's Bush and that he had never taken her to Highway 8. Secondly, that Truscott had ridden Lynne Harper on the crossbar of his bicycle north on the county road toward the bush, the river and to the highway. Then she slipped off of the crossbar and he rode back to the river bridge where he looked back for a last look to see her hitching a ride in a stranger's car.

Huron County Jury Decision: Guilty!

September 30 1959: After listening to 74 witnesses and looking at 80 exhibits over 15 days, the 12-person Huron County jury returned a verdict of guilty of first-degree murder, with mercy. Frank Donnelly represented Truscott and Glen Hays represented the Crown. *Clue 48*

This may be what the jury was thinking when they found **Steven guilty of Lynne Harper's murder: The jury concluded that Lynne Harper died where she was found in Lawson's bush and that she was not picked up at the intersection and subsequently brought back by anyone.** That after passing Gellatly, and before Burns had a chance to see them riding by, Steven left the county road and took Lynne into Lawson's Bush. That is what most witnesses have maintained all along. *(Clue 49)*

If ever a case cried out for rebuttal from the defendant, this was it, yet Steven Truscott did not testify on his own behalf. Throughout the two-week trial he remained detached, watching each witness closely, listening intently to their testimony, keeping his composure; seemingly unworried and self-possessed *(Clue 50)*

Exercising his legal right to silence is all well and good, but *given the overwhelming circumstantial evidence against him, it is difficult to understand how, if he were innocent, any more harm could have accrued had he testified.* (14) Mentally, he was equipped for the task; intelligence and aptitude tests showed him to be a "perfectly ordinary fourteen-year-old boy. (*8, p.44*) *Clue 51*

The evidence is that this incident began when Steven arranged a tentative date with Jocelyne. He wanted a date with a girl that night and he took Lynne when Jocelyne was not available.

No New Trial for Steven Truscott

1960, January 21: A five-judge Ontario Appeal Court sorted out the evidence and came to conclusions as they considered the evidence of the 70 witnesses and 80 exhibits. The Ontario Appeal Court **unanimously dismissed Steven Truscott's appeal on all grounds, saying specifically,** "Toward the end of the trial the learned Judge recharged the jury in these words: 'Let me repeat to you, and it is a matter of fact for you to decide, if you think this evidence is consistent only with the guilt of the accused and inconsistent with any other rational conclusion, you should convict. **But if this evidence or any part of it, whether adduced by the Crown or by the defense, raises a doubt in your mind, a reasonable doubt in your mind, you must acquit him.** *The matter is entirely for you.*'"

Conclusions: The evidence both as to fact and opinion has to be considered as a whole. Our conclusion is that Truscott's evidence on the Reference does not and cannot disturb the finding implicit in the jury's verdict.

That after passing Gellatly, Truscott and Lynne went into Lawson's bush. It is also implicit in the jury's verdict that the girl died where she was found in Lawson's bush and that she was not picked up at the intersection and subsequently brought back dead or alive by someone other than Truscott. *(Clue 52)*

If Truscott **had actually taken Lynne straight to the highway as he told the police and testified before the Supreme Court of Canada, there would be no need for him to tell his friends that, "I was in the woods chasing a cow."** *(Clue 53)*

Sentence Commuted to Life

Truscott had been under a death sentence for less than four months at the Huron County jail. No one believed for a moment that hanging a 14 year old boy would ever happen. (13)

1960 -- January 21: Amid controversy about Truscott's harsh sentence, the conservative Cabinet of Prime Minister John Diefenbaker commutes the sentence to life imprisonment -- not that they doubted the fairness of the trial but, according to cabinet notes, ***hanging a teenage boy would reflect badly on Canada.*** 13

Between 1879 and 1960, there were 438 commutations of death sentences in Canada, including that of Steven Truscott. From 1892 until 1961, the penalty for all murders in Canada was death by hanging. A new act of Parliament divides murder into capital and non-capital categories. Therefore, now only capital murder is punishable by death, which includes planned or violent killings and the murder of police officers and prison guards.

1960: In transit to a new prison Truscott stayed overnight at the Kingston Penitentiary. *(15)*

February 1960 – January 1963: Truscott was incarcerated at the Ontario Training School for Boys in Guelph.

1963: Jan. 14: Truscott (18) moved to Collins Bay Penitentiary.

Chapter 3: 21-year-old Truscott; 25 Witnesses Testify at the Supreme Court

1966

March 24: The first nationwide public interest in Truscott's case came after Isabel LeBourdais' published "*The Trial of Steven Truscott.*" It was the first document to raise serious questions about a young schoolboy who had been sentenced to hang until dead. The hopelessly biased 240-page volume rekindled public debate and incensed many at how badly the justice system had treated Truscott. She argued that the court had erred and sentenced an innocent teen to death. LeBourdais believed Steven was innocent and questioned the police investigation and the trial procedures.

The public outcry and resulting uproar in Parliament led Lester Pearson's liberal government to order a Supreme Court review. *(3)*

April 26:

Saying it is in the public interest that the matter be inquired into; the Canadian Federal Cabinet refers Truscott's case to the Supreme Court over **wide public concerns** that his conviction may have been a **miscarriage of justice.** *(15)*

October 5:

The Supreme Court of Canada decides to hear Truscott's case; not to determine his innocence or guilt but simply whether or not he should have a new trial. *(5)*

Even though a jury of his peers had found Steven Truscott guilty of murdering Lynne Harper in 1959 and the Ontario Appeal Court found that trial to be fair and legal, in 1966

Truscott got a complete review of his case in an unprecedented hearing before Canada's Supreme Court. **Arthur Martin,** considered one of the best criminal lawyers in Canada, represented Truscott. (5)

Isabel LeBourdais and Steven Truscott talk during his Supreme Court Appeal.

1966

In 91 years the Supreme Court had never heard from a convicted felon in person, as they normally review documents and accept briefs. However, *this case had become so politicized;* they decided *to compel direct testimony by asking questions* while watching and listening to the answers from the witnesses. **For the first and only time ever, Truscott had to testify and answer questions from the judges** *about what he did with Lynne Harper.* (5)

Some of the new evidence concerned digestion of stomach contents. Since LeBourdais' book was also published in London, the British publisher sent two premier pathologists, **Professor Keith Simpson for the Crown,** and **Professor Francis Camps** who believed, as did LeBourdais, that Truscott was innocent.

An organized Simpson was better prepared than the flashy Camps who were thought untrustworthy. *(8)* Professor Simpson thought that LeBourdais' criticism of the Canadian Courts, police, and pathologists was biased and unfounded. Meanwhile Camps relied on the evidence in LeBourdais' book that death could have occurred at any time from one to ten hours after eating. Simpson reaffirmed in the strongest possible terms that Dr Penistan, far from being the villain depicted in the Canadian press, had performed his duties honorably and well. At the end **both indicated death could have occurred before 8:00 pm**. *(9)*

Each night Isabel LeBourdais appeared on television to report on that day's court events and to repeat her belief that Truscott was being treated unfairly. Even though, she seemed unable to grasp the fact that it was her distortions, falsehoods, and half-truths that were dragging the name of Canadian justice through the mud, *the public listened to her and ignored the ruling of Canada's Supreme Court. More people listened to LeBourdais' than people who read the Judgment of the Supreme Court.*

Regardless of what LeBourdais said, we start with the proposition that **facts don't lie, so let's stick to the facts**. *(14)*

Timeline – From Missing to Body Found

1959 June: ((Dates are accurate but times are a few minutes either side of the printed time because the events were not important at the time and no child had a time piece.)

This case really begins when Steven Truscott arranges to meet Jocelyne Goddette to show her a calf in Lawson's Bush. The evidence given by Goddette to Justices of the Supreme Court as to her arranged meeting with Steven went as follows: *(15, p. 385)* Clue 54

Timeline of Events; Testifying Before the Supreme Court

Crown: And on ***Monday, June 8th***, Jocelyne did you have a conversation with Steven Truscott?
Jocelyne: Yes, sir.

Crown: Jocelyne, will you tell what that conversation was.
Jocelyne: Well, on Sunday, I had gone to Bob Lawson's barn and saw a calf there. I mentioned that to Steve on Monday, and he asked if I wanted to see two more newborn calves. I said, "Yes". He asked if I could go on Monday and I said: "No", because I had to go to Guides.

Crown: Where were you to go with him?
Jocelyne: Well, he didn't tell me on Monday.

Crown: Well, go ahead.
Jocelyne: And then on Tuesday, he told me if I could go and I told him I didn't know, and **he said to meet him, if I could go, on the right side of County Road just outside the fence by the woods, and he kept telling me not to tell anybody because Bob Lawson didn't like a whole bunch of kids on his property**.

Crown: Now, that conversation is on ***Tuesday, June 9th?***
Jocelyne: *Yes, sir.*

Crown: And when were you to go?
Jocelyne: *Well, at six o'clock.*

Crown: On Tuesday?
Jocelyne: *Yes, sir.*

Crown: Did you see Steven later after school?
Jocelyne: ***Yes, sir.*** **He came to my house about 6:00**, *I didn't answer the door, my brother did, and Steven asked me if we had homework. When he was getting on his bike to leave, I told him I didn't think I could make it because we were starting supper, but that I would try.*

Timeline of Events; Testifying Before the Supreme Court

This evidence was admissible and relevant to establish why Jocelyne said she was looking for Truscott that evening on the county road outside of Lawson's Bush. The subject was deliberately reopened and the following question was put by Crown Counsel to Jocelyne whose answer emphasized the secret aspect of the proposed meeting of the two teens.

Crown: Was there more conversation then on Tuesday?
Jocelyne: *Well, he just kept on telling me to "don't tell anybody to come with you", and that is all.* (5)

Crown: Say that again. He just kept on telling me what?
Jocelyne: *Not to tell anybody.* 5

June 9, 1959, Tuesday

Tuesday, June 9, 1959: Jocelyne Goddette (13) testified that Steven arranged to meet her to see two new calves. *They were to meet just outside the fence by Lawson's Bush at 6:00 pm and she was not to tell or bring anyone. She said Steven came to her house about 5:50, but they were eating so she told him she would meet him later.* (15, p. 386)

6:25 pm: Truscott told the police that after he left home on his bicycle he went first to the school grounds. Finding no one there he rode to the river. **(6:35 pm).** He saw no one at the river so he turned around a couple of times and went back to the station.

(6:55 pm) *Truscott maintains that he met no one on the way down or back.*

On that very hot day, kids from the base had either cycled or walked up County Road to cool off in the swimming hole, which was situated in the Bayfield River, about halfway between Lawson's Bush and King's Highway 8.

630 pm: Paul Desjardine (14), *rode north on his bicycle to go fishing at Bayfield Bridge. He testified that he met Steven a short distance south of Lawson's bush.* They said nothing to each other. Steven was alone and was riding his bicycle around in circles on the county road.

6:35 pm: Mrs. Beatrice Geiger *(32) was riding a bicycle to the bridge when she passed Steven at the bush area riding his bicycle. They were both going north.* Steven went as far as the bridge, stopped a second or two, took a look around and headed south again. She met him the second time at about the railroad tracks. *(5)* **Ronald Demaray** (17) saw Steven in his red pants and distinctive green bike on the bridge and said that he seemed to be just looking around.

After dinner, wearing only turquoise shorts, a white sleeveless blouse and brown loafers, **Lynne Harper** walked to the school grounds where she cheerfully helped **Mrs. Nickerson** with the Junior Guides.

6:40 pm: Kenneth Geiger (12) and **Robb Harrington** were riding double on their way to the river when they saw Truscott sitting on his bicycle in the middle of County Road opposite the "tractor trail" looking towards the station. Kenneth told the police that *Steven said, "Mrs. Geiger was at the bridge" and Kenneth said he knew that.* (15, p. 315) (Clue 55)

6:50 pm: Jocelyne *goes to the bush meeting place but not finding Steven* she cycles to Steve's friend, Bob Lawson at his barn **(7:15)** and *tells him she's looking for Steven*. At **7:25** she leaves saying she's going to look for Steven again.

7:00 pm: Mrs. Nickerson testified that Steven came cycling on the pathway towards them, stopped nearby and sat on his bike. Lynne went over to him and sat on his bicycle fender. They talked for several minutes and then left around the west side of the school. *(Clue 56)* The relevancy of this is that Steven missed his first choice so what girl is likely to accept an invitation on short notice than one willing to go with him? *(15, p315)* Clue 56

7:10:7:15 pm: Steven said Lynne wanted to go to a pony farm just east of County Road on Highway 8. He told the police, "I looked at a school clock and it was about one minute either side of 7:30." He said we pushed the bicycle between us to County Road and she sat on the crossbar and we took off **(7:20).** They cycled north on County Road, past Lawson's bush, and across the bridge. Steven said that **as they rode toward the highway he saw his friends but did not see Burns or Vandenpool. He said that he and Lynne were never in Lawson's Bush.** *(Clue 57)*

7:10 pm: Richard Gellatly and Phillip Burns leave the bridge at the same time, Gellatly on bike and Burns on foot. (15, p. 315)

7:15 pm: Lawson said that Jocelyne was at his barn and asked if he had seen Steven. She stayed about ten minutes.

7:15 – 7:20 pm: Gellatly told police he was riding south on County Road to get his swimming trunks from home when **he met Steven and Lynne between the school and Lawson's Bush riding double on his bike. When he returned a few minutes later he did not see Steven or Lynne.** (15 p. 315)

We know that Steven Truscott and Richard Gellatly passed each other on the county road. The meeting place varies a bit, but always within 100 yards. During interviews on *June 10 and 11, Steven told three different police officers on three different occasions that he passed Gellatly prior to reaching the tractor trail. Gellatly said he met Steven and Lynne at about the brow of the hill. Truscott told F/Sgt. Johnson of the OPP that they met Gellatly a short distance south of the tractor trail and he told Sergeant Anderson that it was "halfway between the school and the bush," which is about where Gellatly said it was. Thursday morning Truscott told RCAF Sgt. Wheelhouse that they met Gellatly* at the crest of the hill between the school and the bush." (15, p. 316 (Clue 58)

7:25: Burns *walking behind Gellatly did not meet Truscott or Lynne,* but he did meet Jocelyn who was cycling fast to the side of the bush closest to the school and she was looking for Steven.

Timeline of Events; Testifying Before the Supreme Court

Meanwhile Steven would tell police that on the way to Highway 8 he waved to friends in the river **(7:40).** In his book he said, *"I took her to the highway, turned around and rode back toward the school."*(7, p.9) **Truscott does not tell us in his book that he did actually drop Lynne off at the highway.** *We would expect him to say that she got off the bike and they had a conversation; at least asking about the pony house or if she would be all right.* **He makes no mention of doing this. Instead, he just turns around and heads back.** *He insists that he dropped Lynne off around 7:40 pm at Highway 8 and when he returned to the bridge "he saw her get a ride with a stranger."* (15, p. 315)

Truscott may have dropped Lynne off, but there is a very good chance he did not drop her off at the intersection. Does he yell to his friends, *"Hey, I just saw Lynne get a ride with a stranger in a new Chevy!"* **No. Does he show guilt that he left a girl friend to an unknown and dangerous fate? No. Does he even tell an adult that a young friend may be in danger!? No.** *(1, 5, 10) Any five year old would have done more.* (Clue 59)

7:25: Jocelyn bikes back to the bush to look again for Steven. *An arranged meeting is the only reason Jocelyne would anxiously be looking for Steven* (Clue 60). She meets Phillip Burns who is walking along the bush area.

7:10 – 7:20 pm: Around 7:10, Teunis Vandenpool (15) rode his bike from their farmhouse on Highway 8 west, turned at the intersection and then south on County Road to go swimming in the river. He did not see a boy or girl on County Road. (*Clue 61*

7:30 – 7:45: Returning home Teunis again was on the clear straight County Road and turned at the intersection. Teunis should have passed by Steven or Lynne, but he **saw no one standing, walking, or riding a bike.** (15) *Clue 62*

(Keep in mind that the Ontario Court of Appeal ruled in 2007 that Truscott and friends can see a car license plate from 1300 feet.)

Timeline of Events; Testifying Before the Supreme Court

7:30 – 7:55 pm: Jocelyne was again looking for Steven outside the bush (about the same time Steve said he was on County Road with Lynne). As Philip Burns and Jocelyne were looking for Steven, Butch George joined in. They called for Steven or Lynne from outside the bush area but failed to find any sign of either. Jocelyne checked one more time at the swimming hole but he was not there either. Disappointed she abandoned her search and for the final time that evening she cycled slowly past the bush right past the body of Lynne Harper about 80 feet in from the road. She shouted Steven's name. She received no answer.

8:00: Jocelyne checked in once more with Bob Lawson for a few minutes and then arrived home before 8:30.

8:05-8:15 pm: Unruffled and not saying anything about the tragic incident he said he had just witnessed, Truscott simply goes back to the school, arriving shortly after 8 pm, where he chats briefly with his brother and friends. When classmate Warren Hatherall saw that Steven had returned to the school without Lynne, he asked, *"What happened to Harper; did you feed her to the fish?" Truscott said that he replied, "No, I just let her off at the highway." There is no evidence that any other remark was made.* (15, p. 322) Does he elaborate on his statement by saying, "I saw Lynne get a ride with a stranger in a brand new Chevy Bel Air!?" No, he does not. *(Clue 63)*

***Does he notify a nearby adult that a very young classmate may be in danger?* Truscott doesn't even notify the girl's father that he just saw his petite little girl hitch-hiking and getting into a stranger's car and head east. What does Truscott do after talking to his brother? He simply goes home to baby sit!** *(Clue 64)*

Timeline of Events; Testifying Before the Supreme Court

8:45 pm – Butch testified that he stopped by Steven's house to talk and play ball and they had this conversation: *(Clue 65)*

Butch: Where have you been all this time?
Steven: Down by the river.

Butch: How come you rode Lynne down there?
Steven: Oh, she wanted a ride down to the highway.

Butch: What was she doing along the bush with you?
Steven: We were looking for a cow and a calf. What do you want to know that for?

Butch: Skip it, let's play ball.

Bob Lawson, a close friend of Truscott, testified that he saw a car near his farm about 10:00 the night Lynn disappeared. A man and maybe a girl were inside. It was very dark.

11:25: Lynne's father reports his missing daughter to base police.

June 10, 1959, Wednesday Morning:

Truscott said that the first occasion on which he knew anything unusual had happened to Lynne Harper was when her father came to the house the following morning, June 10. *(15, p. 324) Clue 66*

Judge: What happened when he came?
Truscott: *He asked me if I had seen Lynne.*

Judge: Did he ask you or did he ask your mother?
Truscott: *I believe he asked my mother and she called me over and I informed him that* "I had given her a ride to the highway."

Judge: Anything else?
Truscott: *I don't remember anything else*.

Judge: Do you remember when the first time you mentioned, if you did mention it, a grey 1959 Chevrolet car to anybody?
Truscott: I don't remember who the first one that I mentioned it.

Judge: Do you remember when you mentioned it, even if you do not remember who you mentioned it to?
Truscott: I believe it was the police. *(15, p. 324) Clue 67*

There is nothing in any records to indicate Truscott had mentioned the car to anyone before telling that story to the police. *In addition, his testimony before the Supreme Court puts him near or in Lawson's Bush on Tuesday evening. They support the contention that Truscott was not candid in describing his whereabouts in his various statements to the police after Lynne disappeared.* *(Clue 68)*

Tom Gillette said that everyone at school was talking about Harper's disappearance and several classmates asked Truscott about Lynne since he was the last person seen with her. Gillette said that while walking into school after recess, *Truscott suddenly remarked that he thought he heard a calf in the woods so he went in to investigate. (Clue 69)*

In Steven's first police interview, before Lynne's body was found, two statements stood out. (1) **He told police officers that he and Lynne passed Richard Gellatly prior to reaching the bush tractor trail.** (2) **He also said that as he and Lynne crossed the bridge he and Butch George waved to each other.** *(Clue 70)*

Three hours later, Steven had his second interview, this time with Constable Donald Trumbley. Steven added that the 59 Chevy had white walled tires and yellow markers in the rear.

June 10, Wednesday Evening:

George Archibald heard Steven Truscott say that he was in Lawson's bush Tuesday evening. This is what he remembered hearing:

Butch: What were you doing in the woods with Lynne?
Steven: I wasn't in the woods with Lynne, was I? *(Clue 71)*

Butch: No, I guess it was somebody else.
Steven: No, I wasn't. I was chasing a cow, wasn't I, **Butch**?

Butch: Yes.

George, Gillette, Paul Desjardine and Bryan Glover all testified about the same conversation:

Paul Desjardine: I asked Butch if Lynne had went into the woods with Steven? Butch didn't say anything, and then I asked Steven if he went into the woods with Lynne, and I said that Butch said you had.

Truscott asked **Butch** if he said that, and Butch said he did not. Then Truscott said *"I was looking for a cow and a calf."*

Glover and **Gillette** also overheard *Truscott say that he was in the bush looking for a calf* on the day Lynne disappeared.

Truscott gave his own version of the conversation among the five boys at the bridge on Wednesday evening, June 10: (15, p. 325)

Judge: Was there any conversation about Miss Harper?
Truscott: *One of the fellows mentioned something about it, yes*.

Judge: Do you remember what it was he said?
Truscott: *He said, "I. heard you had Lynne in the bush".*

Judge: What did you say?
Truscott: *I asked him who had told him this and he said Arnold George did. I went over and asked George and he said he never told anybody that*. *(Clue 72)*

Judge: Were you in the bush with her?
Truscott: *No, sir.*

Judge: Did you make any statement that you were not in the bush; you were at the edge of the bush looking for calves, or anything like that?
Truscott: *No, sir.* (15, p. 325)

Not screaming down the accusations can indicate guilt. These are many damming pieces of evidence against Steven Truscott's stories and actions. *(Clue 73)*

June 10, Wednesday Night:

George: *I had another conversation with Steven:*

Crown: And what was said on that occasion?
George: Well he said that he—like the Police had questioned him and that he had told them that we saw each other down there, and it wasn't me, it was Gordie Logan; and he thought that Gordie was me. And down there at his house he told that to me and he said that the Police were going to go down to my place to check up, so I agreed that I would tell them that I saw Steven down at the river. *(Clue 74)*

June 11, Thursday Morning:

Arnold George backed up Steven with the false alibi and told the police he saw Steven and Lynne pass over the bridge around 7:30 on June 9.

Later that day Tremblay, Truscott, and his mother were at the bridge to verify that Steven could see what he said he saw at the intersection 1300 feet away. When Tremblay told his mother that Steven could not see any licence plates on cars stopped at the intersection she remarked that maybe it was a tourist sticker from a local attraction like they had on their rear fender.

June 11, Thursday Afternoon:

Before Lynne's body was found, several friends were saying that Steven was in the vicinity of Lawson's Bush the evening she disappeared. If every kid is a horrible liar, *each has made up a story putting Truscott near where Lynne's body would soon be found.* We are left with a common sense inference to draw from all this talk about the bush. *If Steven was in the bush that evening, then Lynne Harper was with him.* (*Clue 75*)

There may be no confession of murder in this story, but *the comments Steven makes about taking Lynne into the bush, or being in the bush looking for a calf, come awfully close.* His entire defense is based on the notion that he was not in the bush that evening, yet three independent witnesses heard him say the opposite *before the body was found*. (*Clue 76*)

George testified that around 8:30 pm on Wednesday evening, June 10, he had another conversation with Steven Truscott: (*15*)

Crown: And what was said on that occasion? (*15, p. 322*)
George: Well he said that he...like the police had questioned him and that he had told them that he had seen me down at the bridge, but it wasn't me, it was Gordie Logan. He thought Gordie was me and he told the police that I had seen him. And down there at his house he told that to me and said the police were going to go down to my place to check up, so I agreed I would tell them that I had seen Steven cross over the bridge with Lynne. (*Clue 77*)

George did support Steven's story in his statements to police but after the body was found, he retracted them. In June, 1959, after numerous amendments, George admitted that he had lied to help a friend. Steven had asked him to give a false alibi to back up his story to what he had told the police. (*Clue 78*) After the retraction *every future statement that George told the police and every testimony before the courts was consistent that he did not see Steven cross the bridge with Lynne.* (*5*)

Truscott denied having any conversation with Butch **George** on June 10. He also denied asking George to give the police a false alibi that he had seen Truscott and Lynne at the bridge on Tuesday evening. *(15, p326)* This would be only one of ten denials of seeing, meeting, or talking to friends, classmates, and adults on June 9, 1959. However, **five years later for Bill Trent's book** Truscott suddenly remembers nearly every detail he couldn't recall when testifying before the Supreme Court.

Denials before the Supreme Court

The following people testified that they met Truscott that evening or described his movements and actions on the road between 5:50 and 7.00 pm.

Truscott denied any conversation with **Jocelyne Goddette** about an appointment to go looking for newborn calves in Lawson's Bush. *15, p 326*

Truscott denied that he called at **Jocelyne Goddette's** house around 6:00 pm to confirm their appointment to meet on the county road outside Lawson's Bush.

Truscott denied seeing **Ronald Demaray** who told police that he waved to Truscott at the Bayfield Bridge around 6:30 on June 9th. *(Clue 79)*

Truscott denied that on the trip down to the river between 6 and 7 p.m. that he met **Ken Geiger** and **Robb Harrington**. *5*

Truscott denied seeing **Mrs. Geiger** or **Paul Desjardine** during that trip nor did he remember them giving evidence at his trial.

Truscott denied he met **Ken Geiger** or told him that his mother was at the river. *10, pp 407-8 (Clue 80)*

Truscott denied that he met Richard **Gellatly** on County Road and also did not **remember telling three different police officers that he had met Gellatly just south of Lawson's Bush.** *5, 15*

Truscott denied that he said anything to **Tom Gillette** about being in Lawson's bush on Tuesday evening or about *looking for a calf.*

Truscott denied that Butch was at his house and **he denied** talking with Butch shortly after he returned without Lynne on the night she went missing.

Truscott denied any conversation with **Butch** on June 10.

Truscott denied asking George to give the police a false alibi that he had seen Truscott and Lynne at the bridge on Tuesday evening. (*15, p326*) *Clue 81*

Three Family Friends Testify on Behalf of Steven Truscott

Gordon "Gord" Logan (12), and family friends of the Truscott's said he was fishing from a big rock just by the bend in the river when he saw Steven and Lynne ride by double on Steven's bike. He says he also saw Steven come back alone, stop at the bridge and look back toward the highway. Gordon Logan's evidence was questioned on the ground of credibility and ability to make the observation that he claimed to have made from 642 feet looking into the setting sun.

The Crown concluded that Gord Logan was lying to protect his friend. "*I submit again that Logan is part and parcel with the* **Steven Truscott, Butch George conspiracy.** *I repeat that the evidence is that George was talked into by the accused of telling the Police a false story that he had seen Steven and Lynne going to the highway. I suggest again that Gordon Logan, you can take from the sworn evidence before you, that Gordon Logan got in on the same deal to tell the Police a false story, but unlike George, he has stuck to it.*"*(15 p 321) (Clue 82)*

Douglas Oats (11) said that he was on the Bayfield Bridge on the evening of June 9th looking for turtles when an older boy, Ron Demaray, used his fishing rod to help Karen Daum catch a turtle. Doug said he left the bridge about 7:00 and claims he saw Steven and Lynne go by on his bike about 7:20. Douglas said that he arrived home about 7:30. (15, p. 321)

The prosecution suggested that Doug Oats was mistaken; that on his own admission he saw Steven only once that evening and the time he first gave was a half hour either way of 7:00 pm. So it must have been 6:30, while looking for turtles that Doug saw Steve at the bridge. (Evidence Mrs. Geiger and Demaray) *Clue 83*

The Crown suggests to the jury that Douglas Oates was too bright; too bright, in that he is not to be believed. ***They suggested that Douglas Oats was prepared for a role in defending Truscott, and in doing so he made himself out to be*** a little liar. *(Clue 84)*

To bolster the theory that Oates had lied and that he and Daum had left the area well before Truscott and Lynne could possibly have ridden by, they noted that Desjardine and Mrs. Geiger both saw Oates' and Daum on the bridge around 6:30 p.m. **Truscott was at the bridge at 6:30 and that is obviously when Douglas Oates, Paul Desjardine, and Mrs. Geiger saw him.** (15, p. 321)

After Steven's arrest, new witnesses came forward. **Alan Oats** (16), older brother of Doug, claimed that he went for a ride on his bicycle towards the river on the evening Lynne disappeared. He turned back when he was about 800 feet from the bridge when he spotted Steven wearing red pants alone on the bridge. The time was between 7:30 p.m. and 8:00 p.m.

The Judges also attacked Allan Oats' credibility. Allan said he had evidence highly favorable to Truscott on Tuesday, June 9 but mentioned it only to his mother. He said no one else knew about it until Tuesday, June 16, when Mrs. Durnin approached him at the request of Steven Truscott's father. *(15) (Clue 85)*

It was implicit in the verdict that the jury completely reject both the evidence of those witnesses who said that they had seen Truscott pass over the bridge with Lynne, and Truscott's statements that he saw Lynne enter a car at the intersection.

Supreme Court Decision on the Appeal

1966, October 5 to 1967, May 4: The defense presented new forensic evidence and 21-year old Steven Truscott and 25 other witnesses testified before Canada's Supreme Court. They answered the Judge's questions to the best of their ability. Steven's testimony differed from the other witnesses who described his movements at home and on the road. Parts of Steven's testimony were clearly inaccurate and instead of helping him the inaccuracies contradicted the defence position. *(5) Clue 86*

If Lynne was killed some time after Truscott returned to the school grounds at about 8 pm, the Crown's theory collapsed. Conversely, if Lynne was killed before Truscott returned to the school grounds at about 8 pm, then it was virtually certain that he killed her.

Both Counsels called a total of seven highly-qualified experts who gave evidence pro and con about Dr Penistan's opinion on the time of death. The Court decided that the state of the stomach contents and the weight of the medical evidence **supported Dr. Penistan's opinion that Lynne died prior to 8 pm.** *(5)*

Around 6:30 pm, several witnesses saw Steven riding in circles near the bush entrance in what appeared to be aimless loitering. *The jury most likely considered that this loitering indicated he was waiting for someone and that the person for whom he was waiting was Jocelyne,* who by her subsequent actions indicated that she was looking for Steven at an agreed upon meeting place on County Road near the "tractor trail" and did not find him.

Evidence of the departure time from the school grounds: According to Mrs. Nickerson and Mrs. Bohonus, Truscott had appeared about 7 pm. and left not later than 7.15 pm. On the Reference, Truscott for the first time gave his time of departure as a minute either way of 7.30 pm. (By 7.30 Richard Gellatly and even Philip Burns on foot were home.*5)*

One certainty in this case is that Truscott did meet Richard Gellatly. *Truscott admitted to police officers three different times that he met Gellatly between the school and Lawson's bush. We find it impossible to accept Truscott's statement given before us that he and Lynne left at 7.30 pm.*

Steven did not meet Philip Burns as he should have if he had continued on to the highway. He was not seen by Jocelyne and Arnold George as he would have if he had gone to the highway and returned. The court concluded that after passing Gellatly and before Burns, Jocelyne and George should have seen them, but Steven had disappeared with Lynne into the bush. *(5)*

Decision of Canada's Supreme Court on the First Reference

Answer to the question submitted on the Reference. The government had asked the Supreme Court Justices to determine how it would have decided Truscott's appeal, on the basis of the existing judicial record and any new evidence.

For the foregoing reasons our answer to the question submitted is that had an appeal by Steven Truscott been made to the Supreme Court of Canada, as is now permitted by section 597A of the *Criminal Code* of Canada, on the existing record and further evidence **this Court would have dismissed such an appeal.** *The Supreme Court viewed the conflict between the Crown's County Road evidence that Steven and Lynne disappeared into Lawson's Bush and the defense evidence indicating that they had crossed the bridge and gone to the highway as "the critical issue in this case and entirely a jury problem."*

They concluded that the trial judge properly charged the jury on this critical issue and that the verdict reached by the jury was not unreasonable. *(15, p50) Clue 87*

1967, Feb 24: After a two week hearing the Supreme Court **ruled 8-1 that it would have upheld conviction on the basis that the conduct of the provincial trial was fair and legal.** Eight judges listened carefully to Truscott as he gave his testimony…and they didn't believe a word he said. *(14) Clue 88*

The lone dissenting voice came from Justice E Hall, who wrote "that having considered the case fully, I believe that the conviction should be quashed and a new trial directed. This does not mean I consider Truscott guilty or innocent; that determination is for the jury and for the jury alone."

Justice Hall's recommendation that this case be determined by a jury is surprising by the fact that a jury of his peers had already determined his guilt beyond reasonable doubt. *Further, that jury and Supreme Court Justices had the most knowledge of this crime, and they both found Truscott guilty.*

We have already stated our conclusion that the verdict of the jury reached on the record at the trial ought not to be disturbed. The effect of fresh evidence which we heard on the Reference, considered in its entirety, strengthens that view.

The Judgment of the Supreme Court of Canada: The effect of the sum total of expert witness testimony is, in our opinion, to add strength to the opinion expressed by Dr. Penistan at the trial that the murdered girl was dead by 7:45 p.m.

Steven Truscott believes he can do no wrong; that other people are always the ones at fault. Perhaps Truscott's bad performance *(15, p. 432)* before the Supreme Court gave those eight justices a good reason to find him, well…less than forthright with the truth: The judges watched, listened to, and questioned Steven as he testified and it was clear to them that **his testimony was vague and confused and they did not believe him.**

The fact is that Truscott's testimony differed from the evidence given by the witnesses who described his movements on June 9, 1959.

The new evidence did not cause eight judges to doubt the correctness of the verdict *(15, p. 345-46)*. **The Court returned Truscott to prison to serve out his life sentence.** *(Clue 89)*

In the wake of defeat at the Supreme Court, **Truscott supporter's tried to come up some evidence to support his story.** The *Steven Truscott Defense Committee* placed full-page ads in the *Huron Expositor* appealing to eyewitnesses to come forward. The ad read, "If anyone saw Lynne Harper that evening Truscott can still be proved innocent!" *(Clue 90)* **Result: Not one person saw Lynne**. *(10) (Clue 91)*

Until someone can explain why it is that *Truscott supporters do not accept the testimony of the many people who witnessed the actual events and who knew the most truth about this case. They also testified in courts under oath, something Steven Truscott did only one time and failed miserably.*

Until someone explains why Truscott supporters do not accept the finding of the Ontario Court of Appeal in 1960 that Steven *Truscott's original trial was fair and in accordance with law*.

Until someone can explain why *Steven Truscott supporters ignore the fact that in 1966-7, the Supreme Court of Canada found* 21-year-old *Truscott's testimony before them vague and confused and didn't believe a word he said. (Clue 92)*

Until someone explains *why no one said they saw a boy or girl at the intersection after a full page ad appeared in the Huron Expositor for anyone who saw Lynne Harper that evening to come forward and prove Truscott innocent.* **Not one person has said they saw something that never happened.** *(10)*

Until someone can explain why Truscott's testimony under oath before *Canada's Supreme Court contradicts the testimony of all other witness?* (Except that of his three young family friends)

Until someone can explain why Truscott supporters ignore the judgment of the 1967 Supreme Court whose Justices made it clear that they were *satisfied beyond a reasonable doubt that the facts*, which they found established by evidence which they accepted, *were **not only** consistent with the guilt of Truscott but were inconsistent with any rational conclusion other than that Steven Truscott was the guilty person.*

Until someone can explain why the Ontario Court of Appeal judges were, "*satisfied that Truscott could reasonably believe that he saw the color of the license plate on the vehicle from 1300 feet away*" but not consider in their timeline that his *school-mates could see Steven from 100 feet away.* *(Clue 93)*

Until someone can explain the above seven evidences of guilt, I will have full confidence that Truscott murdered Lynne Harper in Lawson's Bush on June 9, 1959.

1966, Spring:

The first public interest about this case began when journalist **Isabel LeBourdais** published *__The Trial of Steven Truscott__*, the first document to raise serious questions about a young 14-year old schoolboy who had been sentenced to hang until dead. *LeBourdais book came six years after the boy's sentence had been commuted to a life sentence, with possibility of parole.*

1967

Justice Minister PierreTrudeau's cabinet decided not to take any action on the Steven Truscott case at the present time.

Canada's parliament passed a bill placing a moratorium on the use of the death penalty, except in the murder of a police officer, but they did not formerly abolish the death penalty.

Chapter 4: If Steven's Story Were True

The problem arises for Steven Truscott in the stories he tells.

Let's assume that all of Steven Truscott's statements are true. He said that Lynne asked him for a ride to Highway 8 so she could see ponies at the white house nearby. They arrived at the highway one hour before dark. He said that Lynne told him she was annoyed with her mother because she couldn't go swimming, indicating to him that she might run away from home.

Let's take a closer look at Lynne's state of mind. Where does Lynne go after dinner? Does she pack a bag and storm out of the house? Does she run off in tears to her friends and tell stories about her abusive parents? Does she even bother to put on a sweater and stick a toothbrush in her pocket? There are many things we don't know, but we do know that wearing only shorts and a sleeveless blouse, she walks to the school near her home and cheerfully plays "big sister" to the younger Brownies. *(14)*

If Steven's story were true

To the highway, Truscott explains, and within minutes a faceless stranger in a new Chevrolet, like one the Truscott's paper man drove, stops for her, she gets in the front seat, and the faceless man whisks her away. The driver is not described as a bushy haired stranger, or the bogeyman, but he will soon fill both roles.

If Steven's story were true he could tell the police what they talked about as she slipped off his crossbar. He remembered nothing. Evidently, he rode her for 1.2 miles, let her off, and rode slowly back to the bridge without talking about a white house, ponies, hitching a ride or anything else.

If Steven's story were true, when he dropped Lynne off at highway 8 her intentions suddenly change, because she never goes to the little white house to see ponies. **It is one thing for Steven to deny ever taking Lynne into the bush; however, having denied that, he must tell where they went. He was the last known person to see Lynne alive.** *If he didn't take Lynne into the bush, then where did he take her?* **There is no reliable evidence that they were ever near Highway 8.**

If Steven's story were true he would have seen the potential danger in such a tragic event and at least he would yell to his friends that he just saw something terrible happen; that he saw Lynne Harper hitch-hiking and get a ride in a new Chevrolet with a stranger that headed fast down the highway. He might even have told them that I must hurry and tell someone.

If Steven's story were true there would not have been talk among his schoolmates about Steven taking Lynne into the bush, but instead they would wonder why Steven would take Lynne to the highway and leave her all alone at the intersection just one hour before dark.

If Steven's story were true he would have told his brother and classmates at the school yard about what he had witnessed. The time to say something was after he was asked, "what did you do with Harper; feed her to the fish?" Instead, Steven says only that he took her to Highway 8.

If Steven's story were true when he returns to the school alone shortly after 8:00 pm he would want to tell his classmates about Lynne hitching a ride. Even when asked if he fed Harper to the fish, his only reply was that that he took her to Highway 8. Again he said nothing about Lynne getting into a stranger's car.

If Steven's story were true he would have hurried to the girl's home to tell her father that he witnessed Lynne hitch-hiking and get into a car with a strange man that took off fast heading east.

If Steven's story were true he would have told his friend Butch George that night that he took Lynne to Highway 8 and saw her hitch a ride with a stranger in a new Chevrolet Bel Air.

If Steven's story were true he would have told that story to many people before telling it for the first time the next day to the police. George first tells his "in the bush" story to Kenny Geiger and Allan Durnin (10, p. 39) and later that evening to a group of boys at The Custard Cup (10, p. 41-42). Why does he invent a story involving the specific people he sought earlier (Steven and Lynne) being in Lawson's Bush where Jocelyne looks for them earlier if he has no reason to believe they were ever there?

If Steven's story were true he might have apologized and shown a little remorse to Mr. Harper for putting his only daughter into danger. In fact, Steven didn't tell anyone the tragic story about Lynne until her father confronted him the next morning at his house. He did not bother to tell Lynne's father the night before that he saw Lynne hitch-hiking and get into a stranger's car.

We know that Truscott said nothing to anyone about Lynne hitch-hiking or getting a ride with a stranger. Even his own mother and Lynne's father didn't know about his story until after he told it to the police later that morning.

If Steven's story were true, a violent pedophile just happened to be driving on highway No.8 just minutes after he left Lynne all alone. If Steven's pedophile drove on down the road and then decided to rape and kill her, he would most likely have dumped the body miles away from where he may have been seen giving her a lift. Instead, according to evidence, the brainless pedophile turns the car around, drives back to where he picked her up, not at the intersection, mind you, but along a dark trail where he walks 80 feet into a 20 acre woodlot to Steven's favorite place in the bush. There, in the dark, he lays out her socks and shorts in a neat pile, attempts to rape her, decides to strangle her, and then drops her panties 33 feet from the body in the woods. This scenario, like others involving a stranger or a pedophile does not follow a logical path. *(Clue 94)*

A more likely story is that Steven took Lynne into the woods to do what many young boys and girls do in the bushes to become better acquainted. Lynne probably expected a kiss and then back to the school grounds before dark. The evidence is that Lynne, probably while in conversation, took off her brown loafers and set them side by side, removed her socks and rolled them up with care. Perhaps Steven felt they would be more comfortable in a nearby spot so she took her shoes and socks along. Later she took off her shorts, zipped them up, and laid them out neatly as they would be found later. Lynne may have teased too much and gone too far; then tried to get Steven to stop. Now Truscott was too passionate and in no mood to stop.

She may have said she would yell for help or tell on him for trying to rape her. This and his frustration about penetration may have caused him to strangle her. The girl goes limp. In just minutes a 14 year old popular schoolboy has become a killer.

If Steven's story were true Lynne's body would have most likely been found miles away and not in Truscott's favorite place in the bush.

If Steven's story were true, many objective witnesses would have said that they saw Steven riding double with Lynne from the school to the intersection, *not just his three friends.*

If Steven's story were true, he could have gone with other boys to view some newborn calves, but he wanted a girl to go with him, making it difficult to avoid the conclusion that sex was uppermost in his mind. For two days he had pestered Jocelyne to accompany him. When she was not ready, he happened to meet Lynne Harper, who was quite fond of him.

If Steven Truscott's story were true, *someone would have reported seeing Steven or Lynne* at the intersection of County Road and Highway 8. Teunis Vandenpool should have seen them when he rode by there around 7:15 and 7:45 pm on his way to the river and on his return trip home. Not even a random passerby on this busy major highway reported seeing a boy, a girl, a bicycle, or any such sightings at or near the intersection from 7:30 to 8:00 pm on June 9, 1959. If only one person had seen anything this crime case would have reasonable doubt.

Even if Steven's story were true, he would still be held partly responsible for Lynne's death because he took her to a vulnerable spot and left her alone to her fate. If he stayed with the girl and she was picked up, he could be a witness; or perhaps his presence would prevent anything bad happening to her. It matters not; the entire unbelievable story fools no thinking person. *(Clue 95)*

So, *even before Lynne's body* was found there was talk among Steven's schoolmates that he was in the bush the evening she was killed. Truscott maintains that nearly everyone who saw him or said they had a conversation with him was either lying or mistaken. (Some kids, including Butch George, said they were intimidated by his 131lb, 5' 8 ½" physical size. He was respected by his classmates who considered him the biggest, most popular, and most admired kid in class.)

Steven Truscott would add details to his first statements about Lynne hitch-hiking and getting a ride in a new grey Chevrolet. He said he was certain when he saw the chrome and he shape of the fins that the car was a 1959 Bel Air. Also he saw Lynne get into the front seat and that no one was in the back seat.

Fortunately, in the minds of critical thinking Canadians and inquisitive Supreme Court Justices the rendition of events make it a moral certainty and beyond any reasonable doubt that Steven Truscott is the guilty person.

Some crimes get clouded with political and social overtones (such as the death penalty for a juvenile in Truscott's case) and the media plays a key role in public misperceptions of truth.

Death Penalty for Murder Abolished

Before 1962, the only method used in Canada for capital punishment in nonmilitary contexts was hanging. Until now 1,481 people had been sentenced to death, with 710 executed between 1867 and 1962. The last execution was at Toronto's Don Jail on Dec.11, 1962.

1976, July 14: The House of Commons narrowly passed Bill C-84 on a free vote, abolishing capital punishment from the Canadian Criminal Code and replacing it for all first-degree murders with a mandatory life sentence without possibility of parole for 25 years. Between 1879 and 1962 there were 438 commutations of death sentences, including Steven Truscott.

Steven Truscott said that he and Lynne Harper were never there…**except she is there...and she is dead.**

Chapter 5: Media Truscott Campaign

March 24, 1966: The first nationwide public interest in Truscott's case came after Isabel LeBourdais' published *"The Trial of Steven Truscott."* It was the first document to raise serious questions about a young schoolboy who had been sentenced to hang until dead. The hopelessly biased 240-page volume rekindled public debate and incensed many at how badly the justice system had treated Truscott. She argued that the court had erred and sentenced an innocent teen to death. LeBourdais believed Steven was innocent and questioned the police investigation and the trial procedures.

1971

Published by Simon & Schuster, Richmond Hill, Ontario, this 166 page book offers a look at *The Steven Truscott Story* as told to author Bill Trent. **Just 2 years after his prison release, Truscott emerged back into public view to coauthor with Bill Trent his own account of the murder.** *Things Steven could not remember when questioned by Supreme Court Justices* he now clearly remembers for Bill Trent's book.

1979

Pocket Book published, *"Who Killed Lynne Harper?"* Steven Truscott tells his story to author Bill Trent that resulted in renewed interest in the crime. However, non-believers use many of his comments to show that Truscott did kill Lynne. **Truscott criticizes everyone who does not believe his ridiculous story. It is no wonder that he was labeled a narcissist and a compulsive liar.** After a brief flurry of publicity, the case again fades from media attention. *(Clue 96)*

1990's

Truscott might have remained unheralded had not the Canadian legal system been battered all through the 1990's by a barrage of high-profile miscarriages of justice, with compensation payouts soaring after Saskatchewan awarded **David Milgaard** C$10 million for his wrongful conviction of the 1969 murder of nursing aide **Gail Miller**. Suddenly, judicial blunders were big news for readers and viewers and big profits for television and print media.

1997: August 15: *the Fifth Estate*, a CBC documentary program, decided to revisit Canada's most infamous convicted murderer and do a story on Steven Truscott's crime and how his life had been since his release from prison in 1969.

2000: *Until You Are Dead*: *"Steven Truscott's Long Ride into History"*. "The CBC television producer who earned Truscott's trust and helped make a national case of his continued claim of innocence, Montreal's **Julian Sher** presents another compelling indictment of our justice system."

2000, March 29: For nearly three years **Julian Sher** worked with CBC TV's **T***he Fifth Estate* to produce an explosive "documentary" based on his book, *Until You Are Dead*. Truscott is interviewed in the documentary and vows to clear his name. The program unveils what they claim is new evidence to suggest that the police may have been too hasty in pinning the murder on Truscott.

After the CBC broadcast, public clamor to clear Truscott's name grew rapidly sparking a Truscott craze across Canada and questions in Parliament. *Toronto lawyer James Lockyer takes the case. He and DNA evidence had previously overturned Guy Paul Morin's wrongful conviction.*

Chapter 6: Ontario Court of Appeal Rules on Truscott's Convictions

2001

November 28: Lawyers for the Association in Defense of the Wrongly Convicted file a 700-page brief with the federal justice minister to have Truscott's case reopened, as public outcry against the original jury decision grows into Truscott mania.

2002

January 24: Justice Minister **Irwin Cotler** appoints retired Quebec Court of Appeal justice **Fred Kaufman** to assess the case under Section 690 of the Criminal Code. Kaufman can recommend that the case be retried.

2004

April 19: Minister **Cotler** releases the Kaufman 700-page report, saying **there was probably a miscarriage of justice in the Truscott case.**

August:

Kaufman hands his 700 page report to Minister Cotler

October 28 – November 4: Irwin Cotler sends the case to the Ontario Court of Appeal for review to consider if new evidence would have changed the outcome of the 1959 trial. Minister Cotler indicated that Mr. Kaufman of the Quebec Court of Appeal also stated that there is a reasonable basis to conclude that a miscarriage of justice likely occurred in this case. (*16*)

2006

The case against Steven Truscott has already been reviewed to death, with **12 peer jurors and 13 Judges finding him guilty of murdering Lynne Harper on June 9, 1959 beyond any reasonable doubt**. *(Clue 97)*

Even before "new testimony" was presented to the Ontario Court of Appeal, **90% of the public had been persuaded that Truscott had been wrongly convicted.** After reading the biased books, seeing one-sided TV shows, and reading simple thoughts from reporters and commentators, most Canadians are convinced that Truscott did not murder Lynne Harper. *Clue 98*

Many people who have never read anything objectively about this case have intergraded themselves into the media's fantasy bogeyman, usually an Army pedophile. *The notion that the RCAF would frame a 14-year old boy in order to let a homicidal pedophile run free is frankly too absurd for comment.13)* *Clue 99*

As the Ontario Court of Appeal reviews Truscott's conviction, **there is no mention about Truscott's testimony before the Supreme Court of Canada in 1966. It's like it never happened at all. What gives here? After a two week hearing, eight of our Supreme Court justices essentially call Steven Truscott a liar,** yet the firestorm of public opinion seems to be overwhelming that the man is innocent and wrongly convicted. Were Isabel LeBourdais' nightly TV talk shows during the Supreme Court hearing more successful in moving public opinion than the actual judgment of the Supreme Court?

Inquisitive Canadians who objectively read a great deal about the Truscott case were shocked that **in none of those accounts is there any mention about Truscott's testimony before the Court in 1966 at which eight Supreme Court justices essentially call Steven Truscott a liar.**

The 1967 Judgment of the Supreme Court of Canada read as follows: "The verdict of the jury makes it clear that **they were satisfied beyond a reasonable doubt that the facts,** *which they found to be established by the evidence, were not only consistent with the guilt of Steven Truscott but were inconsistent with any rational conclusion other than that Steven Truscott was the guilty person."*

History shows that some children not only have the ability to kill, they also can hoodwink adults. Had it not been for his age, Steven Truscott would now be some half-forgotten sex-killer, and Isabel Le Bourdais would not have written her strong faulty opinions that escalated from a senseless teen tragedy into a full-blown "miscarriage of justice".

Fortunately, until 1998, cooler heads and objective critical thinkers were on hand to undermine the rhetoric and expose *the Pro-Truscott campaign for what it really was – a* **"miscarriage of truth".** (*Clue 100)*

April 6: Lynne Harper's remains are exhumed from her grave in southwestern Ontario with her family's consent. The order to exhume was made by the Attorney General of Ontario to test for DNA evidence and hopefully to bring closure to the case without further court hearings.

April 10: Ontario's chief coroner announces that **medical examiners are unable to find any useable DNA evidence on the exhumed body of Lynne Harper.**

Testimony Presented to Ontario Court of Appeal at Osgoode Hall in Toronto

June 19: Ontario's chief pathologist **Dr. Michael Pollanen** casts doubt on the exact time when Lynne Harper died. An original autopsy concluded that Lynne died in the early evening but Dr. Pollanen testified there wasn't enough evidence to draw that conclusion. **He said that she could have died during the time Truscott says he was with her or the following day.**

2006

June 21: Pathologist **Dr. Werner Spitz** testified that Dr. John Penistan, the original pathologist who looked at Harper's autopsy in 1959, was advanced, but said, "Maybe he was wrong." **But Spitz testified that he stood behind Dr. Penistan's findings.**

June 22: Retired Ontario Provincial Police Superintendent **Harry Sayeau** told the court that he and his colleagues did not seek out other suspects in 1959. He testified they didn't inquire about sexual predators with other nearby Ontario Provincial Police, Crown offices, or the Royal Canadian Air Force.

June 26: Two experts present conflicting entomology evidence, which uses the larval development of bugs to estimate the time of a person's death.

Dr. Neal Haskell, a Purdue University forensic entomology professor told the court that larvae must have been deposited on Harper's body before sunset on June 9, 1959, between 9 and 9:30, meaning **Lynne could have died between 7:15 and 9:30 pm**.

Elgin Brown, a biologist working at the crime lab of the Ontario attorney general testified that maggots found on Harper's body were in the first stage of development and laid the next morning.

June 28: Sandra Stolzman and Elizabeth Hulbert testified that Jocelyn Goddette, a key child witness in Truscott's 1959 trial, told fellow nurses in Montreal in 1966 that she lied under oath.

June 29: Sarah VanLaerhoven, Entomologist at Windsor University tells the Ontario Court, "that her review suggests it's likely she was killed after sunset on the 9th but before 7 am on the 10th." Under cross, **VanLaerhoven admits she cannot rule out that Lynne could have died before sunset on June 9th.**

June 30: Bob Lawson, the farmer who owns the property where Harper's body was found, testified he saw a strange car parked near his fence line about 10:00 pm the night the 12-year-old disappeared. Lawson told the court he reported the incident to the guardhouse at the Clinton AFB, but the officer on duty was not interested. Lynne's father reported her missing at 11:20 pm.

July 5: For the Crown, Karen Jutsi (maiden name Daum), who was nine years old when she testified in the 1959 trial, said her statement was reported incorrectly. Karen was reported as saying that she was on the bridge when she saw Steven and Lynne on County Road sometime after 7 pm on June 9. Now she tells the court that she was not on the bridge, but was near Lawson's bush.

Karen said she was shocked when she read the clearly wrong statement. Karen was a Truscott witness in the first trial but now says she did not see Truscott at the bridge. Karen's original testimony may have been coerced by Defense.

July 6: Dr. Nicholas Diamant, Professor of Medicine at the University of Toronto told the court that emotional stress can stop digestion for several hours and that in a normal person it can take up to six hours for food to leave the stomach. Since there was still food in her stomach **the defence pathology evidence shows that the opportunity window could have extended to darkness on June 9.**

Renowned United Kingdom Pathologist **Bernard Knight** questioned key forensic evidence used to convict Steven Truscott in 1959. The Pathology professor criticized Doctor Penistan's use of stomach content analysis to estimate the time of Lynne Harper's death.

Then as now, the crime scene continues to support the Crown's theory. Not one pathology or entomology expert ever testified that Lynne could not have died before 8:00 pm when Truscott was with her. The "fresh" evidence does not exclude the possibility that Truscott was the killer. *(15)*

Steven Truscott Acquitted

2007, Jan. 31–Feb 14: Lawyers for Truscott and Ontario's Attorney General make their final arguments before the five appeal court judges. To satisfy the public, television cameras are allowed into the appeal court for the first time and proceedings are broadcast live. The lawyers and each judge can now be seen, heard and evaluated individually so that Canadians and other English speaking people around the world can scrutinize each judge and hold him responsible for a "wrong decision". Most Canadians knew that a guilty verdict would have been tragic, possibly resulting in riots in the streets.

OCA: *Quotes from the <u>Ontario Court of Appeal</u>*
SDM: Comments by **Sam Dennis McDonough**

Aug. 28: More than 48 years after the crime and after every court denied appeals, the Ontario Court of Appeal overturns Truscott's conviction, declaring the case "a miscarriage of justice that must be quashed." The Court is satisfied that the new material before this court has undermined the ***Crown's four factual pillars:***

OCA: *First, on the issue of the time of Lynne Harper's death, the pathology evidence that we have admitted as fresh renders the medical evidence heard in prior judicial proceedings, to the effect that Lynne must have died before 8 pm on June 9, scientifically untenable.* We also think that it would be open to the jury at a new trial to find that the appellant's entomology evidence, together with the pathology evidence raises a reasonable doubt as to whether Lynne Harper died before 8:00 pm on June 9. That doubt would require the acquittal of the appellant. In so holding, we stress that it is not incumbent on the appellant to prove that Lynne Harper probably died after 8:00 pm; only that death after 8:00 pm was a reasonable possibility. We are satisfied that the entomology and the pathology evidence meets this standard.

SDM: Both the prosecution and the defense presented pathology and entomology experts. Some backed Dr. Penistan's original findings; some refuted them and the methods he used. However, the trial of his peers and three court appeals had credible evidence presented before them that Lynne most likely died within the 2 ½ after eating supper around 5:30 pm. No expert testified that Lynne Harper could not have died before 8:00 p.m.

OCA - The County Road evidence: *As for the second pillar of the Crown's case, in the "Burns-Gellatly" cornerstone the archival material suggests that a credible case could be made that Philip Burns and Richard Gellatly did not leave the area of the bridge at the same time and proceed in tandem southbound on the County Road. At the same time, the archival material suggests an alternative theory that is consistent with the Court's position that Truscott left the school around 7:20 p.m. and took Lynne on his bike along the county road to highway 8 unseen.*

The Appeal Court acknowledges that this timing is somewhat inconsistent with Truscott's sworn testimony before the Supreme Court in which he stated that he and Lynne left the school grounds "one minute either way of 7:30 pm." The Appeal Judges prefer the earlier time of 7:20 p.m. because it is largely consistent with some of Truscott's statements that he gave to the police.

SDM: *Steven Truscott, in most of his interviews, said that as they were leaving he looked at the school clock which showed 7:30. Two reliable independent witnesses testified that Steven and Lynne left the school between 7:00 and 7:10, but not later than 7:15 pm.* **The Ontario Court Justices found that exactly 7:20 pm would best satisfy Truscott's stories of taking her to the highway and be seen only by his friends crossing the bridge.** That is not necessarily true because the kids could see 1300 feet down the straight narrow County Road and would have seen the pair if they were actually there. *15 (Clue 101)*

OCA: *As for the third pillar of the Crown's case, in the county road evidence, that pillar could be significantly weakened by the archival material which provides support for the claim that Truscott could reasonably believe that he saw the color of the license plate on the vehicle while standing on the bridge 1300 feet away. 15*

SDM: **This very court ruled that Steven Truscott can see an automobile license plate from 1300 feet. Following their line of we can assume that his classmates could see a tall boy with red pants riding double with a girl from 1300 feet away.**

Their inability to see Steven has only one explanation: He could not be seen because he turned off County Road and took Lynne to his favorite place in the bush. Several people would have seen Steven and Lynne riding toward the intersection, if only they had done so. No one, not a bright eyed witness on the road, not even Truscott's three young witnesses ever reported seeing Steven or Lynne at or near the County Road and Highway 8 intersection on June 9. *Clue 102*

No driver passing by on this major highway reported seeing a girl or a girl and boy standing at or near the intersection during the time Steven says they were there. They had vanished, only to find one would soon return and the other would be found dead near where both were last seen. *15*

OCA: *The penis lesions evidence: The fourth pillar of the Crown's case, the **penis lesions evidence** that so vividly demonstrated Truscott's guilt at trial has been weakened to the extent that it is virtually no evidence at all.*

SDM: Dr. Addison testified that the distal end of Truscott's penis appeared swollen and slightly reddened. He observed two large raw sores oozing serum that were roughly the size of a quarter and were "like a brush burn of two or three day's duration." (*15, p.604*)

More importantly, *the lesions on the girl, the damage to the hymen and the entrance are injuries that are consistent with a boy, who is really a man, in his attempt to have intercourse with a 12-year-old child.* *(15, p.605*)

Steven Truscott explains the injuries to his penis: *(Clue 103)*

First he says it was from his zipper.

Then he suggests it was masturbation. *(15, p.605)*

Then in his own 1979 book he claims it was a rash that began six weeks earlier and was much smaller than the doctor's said.

Then in the 2000's, Truscott claims there were not any marks ever.

It makes no sense for so many people believe that every kid and adult in this story is a liar except Steven Truscott.

OCA: *For these reasons we have concluded that, while it cannot be said that no jury acting judicially could reasonably acquit, we are satisfied that if a new trial were possible, an acquittal would be the more likely result. Accordingly, in the words of [s. 696.3(3) (ii) of the Criminal Code] the appeal is allowed, the conviction for murder is set aside and an acquittal entered.*

SDM: Evidence, as to fact and opinion must be considered as a whole; not to pick and choose evidence to fit the decision. It appears that the Ontario Appeal Court, under duress from the media and the public, chose to forego objective critical thinking of the whole evidence. They were bound and determined to acquit Steven Truscott and would try to prove their openness by televising the entire show nationwide.

Why did Ontario Court Justices work for the Defense and against the Crown? They had no choice. When judges or politicians face a high degree of clamoring from the voting public they will find a way to appease. Why fight the maddening crowd? *So, the Court of Appeal allowed "fresh evidence" from the defense in order to acquit Truscott, even though the Crown's solid position was that there was no "new" or "fresh" evidence. It seems that the only real purpose of the Ontario Appeal Court was to find reasons to acquit Truscott, appease the public's Truscott craze, and prevent riots in the streets.*

In not finding Truscott innocent the Ontario Court of Appeal wrote, "**Before the Court of Appeal, Truscott sought not only an acquittal but an affirmative declaration of his innocence." The Court declined to issue a declaration of innocence.** *It was of the view that Mr. Truscott had not, in fact, demonstrated his innocence...certain immutable facts casting suspicion on Mr. Truscott...***in particular, the fact that he was the last person known to have seen Lynne Harper alive, and the fact that he was with her close to the location where she was murdered – made demonstrating his innocence particularly difficult."***(Clue 104)*

Compensation for Steven Truscott

2008, April 16: Guelph Member of the Provincial Parliament (MPP) Liz Sandals tables a private members' motion for compensation for Truscott. All parties support the motion.

2008, July 7: The Ontario government announces it will pay Truscott $6.5 million in compensation for his ordeal. Michael Bryant, former Ontario Attorney General tells reporters that the Crown has no plans to appeal and offers Steven Truscott an apology. As for Attorney General Michael Bryant's statement on the case, **Truscott commented, "I know he apologized on behalf of the government. But I don't really feel that the apology was sincere."**

Chris Bentley, Ontario's Attorney General said, "We are doing what we can to bring to the conclusion this remarkable aspect of Mr. Truscott's life's journey. Bentley went on to say Ontario is paying it now in full to ensure Truscott is compensated quickly."

Ordinarily, Canada does not pay compensation when there is no *affirmative declaration of innocence*. Truscott, however, calls the Ontario's C$6.5 million compensation for his prison time and murder conviction "bittersweet." He says money will never truly pay back the years of his life lost while in prison. **Truscott's wife received C$100,000 and the federal/province paid C$990,000 in legal aid bills. Truscott's compensation calculates to over C$75 for each hour he was in jail or prison.**

Truscott's Ride through History

Steven's classmates said young Steven was a tough, cool kid. Today Mr. Truscott has shown himself to be a clever, devious man. For those who think a 14 year old boy could not have killed his 12 year old classmate and remain calm and collected should consider this: **Anyone who can convince authorities and the public to reduce his sentence from hanging until dead to ten years and freedom, and then rally tax-payers to give him C$6.5 million dollars for a crime he committed and found guilty is capable of raping and killing a little 12 year old girl. Oh Canada has been duped, hoodwinked, and swindled by a money-hungry media and a smart, gutsy guy.**

What kind of person can act normally within hours after killing someone; a person who can kill one hour, show calmness and act normally with friends the next? The answer is: **A person with an antisocial personality, manifested in aggressive, perverted, criminal, or amoral behavior without empathy or remorse and unable to feel guilt for such acts. In one word a *psychopath*.**

Perhaps the Steven Truscott case had such notoriety that the Ontario Court of Appeal felt they had no choice but to acquit Truscott and give him a large payment. If not acquitted the public would be in a frenzy, the media would be ready to pounce, and the world would watch in horror and disbelief. Indeed, the world was watching and were elated when the convicted killer was awarded $C6.5 million for his crime.

From the *London Free Press* after the verdict: *It would be regrettable indeed if public emotionalism and hysteria was permitted to denigrate or subvert our judicial processes.*

From the *Toronto Daily Star: As always...the Truscott case was more about politics than it was about law.*

We can't blame Steven Truscott for taking advantage of a tragic event. In 1964 he knew why he was in prison when in wrote on his parole application, *"If I were released I would not be in trouble again. I have paid five years of my life but this has taught me that crime does not pay, so all I ask is please grant me one chance to make a success of my life and prove that one dreadful mistake does not mean that I will ever make another one."*

Until someone can explain why *Steven Truscott supporters ignore the fact that in 1966-7, the Canada Supreme Court found* 21-year-old *Steven Truscott's testimony before them vague and confused and didn't believe a word he said.*

Truscott said, "This was the first news I received that a stay of execution had been ordered. I was dazed and it was some time before the full significance of what had occurred got through to me. I wasn't going to die!" **Perhaps there would be yet another miracle, an appeal, a new trial, even an acquittal."**

An innocent person would consider a stay of execution the right thing to do, not a miracle. An innocent person prays that whoever killed the victim will be caught and confess.

Chapter 7: Questions and Answers that Show Who Killed Lynne Harper

Q: Why did Steven Truscott propose a secret date with Jocelyne Goddette to see calves in the woods, and then tell her not to tell anybody and not to bring anyone?
A: If Steven only wanted to see calves with someone, he could ask his best friend, Butch George, or any other boys his age. He arranged to meet Jocelyne by Lawson's woods to show her a calf, or whatever boys and girls do in the woods.

"I arrived home about 5:30. Supper was late and Mom asked me to buy coffee at the store. **I would have to hurry because it closed at six."** *(7, p.8)*
A: Truscott is not telling us that he did hurry. He is saying that he *should* hurry. These changes in tenses show us that he had plans between 5:30 and 6:00 besides going to the store. What else was going on shortly before 6:00 pm? 12

Truscott: *"Then Crown called what it considered its key witness, a 13-year-old girl named* **Jocelyne Godette** *who was also in my class, and* **her testimony really infuriated me. She testified that early on the day of the murder I had made a date with her to look for newborn calves in Lawson's bush. She said further that between 5:30 and six that day, I had gone to her house to collect her but, not having had supper, she was unable to accompany me. She said that I wanted to go to the place where they found Lynne. At the time she had me at her house, I was buying coffee for my mother."** *(7, p.36)*
A: Jocelyne's statements would infuriate Steven only if they were true.

Q: Why did Jocelyne not agree to meet Steven until later?
A: Jocelyne was about to eat a late supper, and she may have been playing hard to get.

Q: Why was Steven riding around aimlessly near the bush area? **A:** The evidence is that **Steven was waiting anxiously for Jocelyne at their agreed meeting place outside the bush.**

Q: Why did Steven bike back to the school to seek out Lynne?
A: Perhaps he tired of waiting for Jocelyne. At a party the previous Friday, Lynne showed interest in popular Steven and asked him to dance, which they did for awhile. *(Clue 105)*

*"I rode to the school where I met a group of Brownies. After I followed the county road to the bridge, stopping briefly here and there, I went back to the school where I met Lynne. We chatted a while about...**Well, who remembers what we talked about?** She was in a chatty mood and did most of the talking." (p. 8)*
A: Perhaps Truscott remembered but didn't want to say if he and Lynne talked about desires and personal things. Truscott starts to tell us what he and Lynne talked about, but then changes his mind and chooses not to reveal this information. He does not tell us that he doesn't remember their conversation. He alludes to having a memory loss by stating, "Well, who remembers what we talked about?" Since he is the last person known to see Lynne alive, what they discussed prior to her death is of utmost importance to the police and everyone else. *12*

Q: Why did Steven ride Lynne on his bicycle crossbar?
A: Steven says he ran into Lynne on the school grounds and she was in a chatty mood. Keep in mind that **no one heard Lynne ask for a ride, that was just Truscott's story. Perhaps Lynne wanted to go where she might get a kiss or two and then return to the school grounds.**

77

Q: Why did Steven give different times for when he left the schoolyard with Lynne?
The time? "It was probably between 7:30 and 7:45" *(7, p.8-9)*
and, ***It was shortly after 7:00.*** *(10)*
and, ***While leaving I saw the Kindergarten clock at 7:25.*** *(5)*
and, ***The school clock said a minute either way of 7:30.***
A: Truscott was trying to figure the time that would best satisfy his story. *(Clue 106)*

"She wanted a <u>lift</u> to the highway and I gave it to her. Then she said she wanted to see the ponies and asked if I would take her to the intersection. I agreed and <u>we</u> pushed the bicycle between <u>us</u> across the school grounds to the county road. There I got on the seat and she mounted the crossbar and <u>we</u> took off. The time?...Probably between 7:30 and 7:45 pm." *(7, p.8-9) (Clue 107)*

The pronouns "we" and "us" indicate a partnership. All we know for sure is the "partnership" was pushing the bike across the school yard and riding away double with Steven's arms around Lynne as she sat on the crossbar. (*12)*

Q: Why was Lynne in a friendly, chatty mood while riding on the cross bar of Steven's bike?
A: She was probably thrilled that a popular, athletic 14-year old boy would pay attention to her.

Q: Why did the *Fifth Estate* movie show Lynne riding on the handle bars instead of on the crossbar as was testified in the Courts by Truscott and every witness who saw them? *(11)*
A: The biased program did not want to show Lynne happily riding on the crossbar with Steven's arms around the girl.

Q: Why was Jocelyne looking near Lawson's bush for Steven?
A: Steven told Jocelyne to meet him on County Road at Lawson's Bush. There was no other reason for Jocelyne to be searching for Steven at that time in that place. *8*

"I took her to the highway, turned around and rode slowly back toward the school." (*7, p.9*)
A: Truscott does not tell us in his book that he did actually drop Lynne off at the highway. **We would expect him to say that she got off the bike and they had a conversation. Perhaps he asked her if she would be all right or where the house was with the ponies. However, he makes no mention of doing this. Instead, he just turns around and heads back. He may have dropped Lynne Harper off, but there is a very good chance he did not drop her off at the intersection.** *12 (Clue 108)*

At first Truscott said that when he returned to the bridge he was seen by Arnold George and Douglas Oaks. Does he say to his friends, "I just saw Lynne get a ride with a stranger in a brand new Chevy Bel Air!?" No. He doesn't even feel guilty that he left his girl friend to an unknown and dangerous fate. Does he even bother to notify an adult that a very young classmate may be in danger? No. *(1, 5)*

Q: While returning to the school a classmate asked Truscott, *"What did you do with Harper, feed her to the fish?"* *"I replied that I had taken her and let her off at Highway No. 8."*

A: Warren Hatherall had seen Steven riding double with Lynne toward the bush and he was curious as to why Steven came back alone. **When the police asked Truscott whether his schoolmates made any comment to him after his return to the school, he replied: "I believe one of them asked me, 'What did you do with Harper, feed her to the fish?' and I replied that I had taken her and let her off at Highway No. 8."**

Q: When Truscott returned to the school grounds his classmates testified that he appeared normal, calm as always; he did not appear bruised, anxious, or sweaty.

A1): **The same classmates also did not report seeing the rip in the seat of his jeans, at the top of his right leg or the stains on both knees. In addition, he did not tell them that he saw Lynne hitch a ride with a stranger.** *5 (Clue 109)*

A2: Truscott did not bother to stop by the home of Lynne's parents to tell them that he saw their daughter hitch-hiking on King's Highway or that he saw her sped away in a stranger's brand new car.

Q: What kind of person can act normally within hours after killing someone?
A: A person who can kill one hour, show calmness and apathy and act normally with friends the next hour. A person with an antisocial personality disorder, manifested in aggressive, perverted, criminal, or amoral behavior without empathy or remorse and who is unable to feel guilt for such acts. In one word a *psychopath.*

Q: Why would Butch invent a story involving Steven and Lynne at the bush if he had no reason to believe they were there?
A: Perhaps Butch heard about Steven riding with Lynne and since he had not seen them on the road he figured they were in the bush. Also, Butch looked for them with Jocelyne at the place she was to meet Steven. She had no other reason to be there and the searches had no reason to look anyplace else.

Q: Why did the Clinton base security not investigate people in the car seen near Lawson's farm?
A: Truscott's friend, Bob Lawson reported the incident to base security on June 12, three days after she went missing.

Q: Why did the police not seriously consider the fresh set of tire skid marks leading out of Lawson's Bush onto the county road?
A: It was considered but the timing did not fit logically into the evidence already found. All of the evidence is presented fully in this book.

Q: Why did Lynne's parents consider that their daughter may have hitched a ride to her grandmother's house?
A: It probably **never occurred to them that anything tragic could happen to anyone in their rural, close-knit, friendly surroundings on the air force base. They may have been searching for every possible answer to where she could be.**

Truscott: *"The first knowledge I had that something unusual had happened to Lynne was the morning after our bicycle ride. She wanted a lift to the highway and I gave it to her."*(7.139)
A: Had Truscott forgotten his story that he saw her get into a stranger's car the night before? Most people would consider that unusual. In addition, by using the pronoun "our" the bicycle ride becomes more personal than just giving her a lift. Describing it as "our bicycle ride" he is telling us this ride meant more to him, and possibly to her. 12

Q: What is the evidence that Truscott and Gellatly met prior to reaching Lawson's Bush?

A: Truscott told F/Sgt. Johnson and Sgt. Anderson of the OPP on Wednesday, June 10, 1959 and to Sgt. Wheelhouse of the RCAF and Constable Hobbs on Thursday morning, before Lynne's body was found, that he had met Gellatly "halfway between the school and the bush," going north. Richard Gellatly confirmed that they had met and passed each other about the time mentioned by both.

Q: Why did Truscott tell the police, *"I hardly knew the girl I kept trying to tell them? We were classmates but she was not among my friends. What she did outside school, and inside it, too, for that matter, had never interested me." (7, p 16) (Clue 110)*

A: In talking to the police, Steven down-plays his relationship with Lynne Harper. Classmate, Lorraine Wood said that at her birthday party on the previous Friday, June 5, Lynne asked the popular Steven to dance with her and they did for a short time. Everyone knew that she was fond of Steven. *12*

"I was in the woods chasing a cow." Steven Truscott

A: One day before Lynne's body was found Butch George asked Steven what he was doing in the woods with Lynne. At first Steven denied being in the woods, but shortly after said *he was in the woods chasing a cow.* 5

Q: Why did Arnold (Butch) George lie to the police at first but later tell the truth and always testify truthfully?

Butch George: On Wednesday evening, June 10 (one day after the murder and one day before Lynne's body was found) I had a conversation with Steven.

Supreme Court Judge: And what was said on that occasion?

George: Well he said that he—like the Police had questioned him and that he had told them that we saw each other down at the river, and it wasn't me, it was Gordie Logan; and he thought that Gordie was me. And down there at his house he told that to me and he said that the Police were going to go down to my place to check up, so I agreed that I would tell them what he had told me to say.

However, when Lynne's body was found George realized that helping a friend can go just so far. Soon he told the police the truth that he did not see Steven. Afterward George always testified the truth. *15*

Questions and Answers about Truscott's Case

Q: *Yesterday evening I heard a calf in the woods and I went in to investigate." Steven Truscott*

A: On Wednesday evening, the day before Lynne's body was found, Steven Truscott tells Tom Gillette that he heard a calf in the woods the prior evening and he went in to investigate. *5*

Q: What was the condition of Truscott's underpants that were taken off of him at the time of his arrest?

A: They were dirty and showed traces of blood and male sperm. The red trousers taking from his home had been washed but still showed stains on both knees and a rip on his right leg pant. *(5, 15)*

Q: What did two doctors find on Steven's body the day of his arrest?

A: Doctor J. A. Addison and an Air Force doctor found scratches on Truscott's torso and two raw lesions the size of quarters on either side of the shaft of Truscott's penis. They testified that raping a small virgin could have caused the sores and said the wounds corresponded with damage found in Lynne's genital area. *(5, 15)*

Q: Why was Lynne Harper the victim in this case?

A: If it were not for the murder of Lynne Harper, the incident would mean no more than Steven had a tentative date arranged with Jocelyne Goddette. The evidence is that **Truscott wanted a date with a girl that evening and he took Lynne when Jocelyne seemed not to be available.**

Questions and Answers about Truscott's Case

Q: Isn't Julian Sher's suggestion that Steven's hitchhiking story is credible because Lynne had hitchhiked in the past with friends to go shopping or to the skating rink? (10, p. 22)

A. Take a closer look at the details and it becomes clear that we have an entirely different situation that night. Lynne Harper is alone, it is a school night, it is getting late, she wears only her summer clothing, she carries little or no money, she tells no one about her plans, and she has no real reason to suddenly leave home. *(Clue 111)*

Q: Why did the police not have Steven's father with him during the interrogation.

A: In 1959, the Juvenile Delinquents Act did not require a youth's parent or guardian to be present during a police interview. *(15)*

At the Goderich OPP station, Inspector Harold Graham from the Criminal Investigations Bureau, assisted by Constable Trumbley, interviewed Steven for an hour and a half

Graham: It is difficult for me to understand how you could see what you say you saw at the highway from the bridge because the distance is so great. Are you sure that what you have told us is what you actually saw?
Steven: Yes.

Graham: Are you sure that you saw Lynne with her thumb out at the highway?
Steven: Well, I didn't actually see her thumb; only her arm.
Truscott said, "I stuck to what I had said."

Questions and Answers about Truscott's Case

Q: What are some other reasons why Truscott's story about Lynne hitch-hiking is a lie? *(Clue 112)*

A1: Lynne would not go 1.2 miles to the highway to hitch-hike alone at 7:30 pm if she had to be home by 8:30 pm.

A2: Lynne was wearing shorts, a sleeveless blouse and loafers. Even on a summer evening this is no outfit for hitch-hiking.

A3: Steven said that Lynne wanted a ride to the pony farm. Since it was getting late and he had already taking her 1.2 miles, why not take Lynne .3 miles further to the farm?

A4: Another Truscott story was that Lynne told him she was upset with her mother and she wanted to hitch a ride to her grandmother. But two adults said Lynne was cheerfully helping them with the younger children, and even Steven said she was in a chatty mood while riding on his bicycle crossbar.

A5: What possible sense does it make for this child to walk over and help the Clinton Brownies if she is planning all along to hitchhike eighty miles to visit her grandmother?

A6: Lynne did not have the disposition or desire to run away or to hitch-hike at 7:30 when she had to be home by 8:30.

A7: If we believe Truscott, then we have to believe that this kid was soon planning to leave her home and her parents and head east with the first stranger who picked her up.

A8: Perhaps it was Truscott's kindness that caused him to give his young girl friend a ride. Unfortunately, this character of kindness was unable to wait a few minutes until the little girl hitched a ride. **If he had been with or near Lynne when she got a ride the driver would have known that there would be a witness if anything happened to her.** (Perhaps Steven was in a hurry to meet up with his other girlfriend. It matters not because the evidence shows that Truscott made up the hitch-hike story.)

Questions and Answers about Truscott's Case

A9: On this major fairly busy highway it is highly likely that several cars passed by the intersection during the time they were there and when Steven said Lynne was hitch-hiking. If anyone had seen either of them they would have reported it to authorities in this high profile case.

A10: Evidence is that not one person ever reported seeing Lynne or Steven Truscott at or near the intersection, simply because they were never there. If even one person passing by that intersection had seen a boy or girl, there would be no arrest of Steven. There would be no reason for this book in search of truth because now there would actually be reasonable doubt. **The truth is…they simply were not there.**

A11: Gordon "Gord" Logan (12), family friends with the Truscott's, was fishing in the river. Let's say that Gord really did see Steven and Lynne on their way to the highway and saw Steven return alone, stop at the bridge and look back toward the highway. **Did a surprised Truscott yell to his friends that he just saw Lynne get a ride with a stranger in a brand new Chevrolet and that she may be in danger? There is no evidence that he did.**

A12: Evidence is Truscott said nothing to his friend Gord.

A13: When he returned to the school did Steven Truscott say anything about Lynne getting a ride quickly and in a brand new car? No, he did not. The evidence is that when Truscott was asked if he fed Lynne to the fish his soft reply was that he took her to Highway 8. He did not say that Lynne was brave to get into a car with a stranger or that she could be in danger.

A14: He failed even to tell Lynne's father about seeing his young petite daughter getting a ride in a carwith a stranger.

Questions and Answers about Truscott's Case

Q: Why was Steven's statement about taking Lynne to the highway where he saw her hitch a ride considered not a true story by the jury? *(Clue 113)*

A1: If Steven had stayed with Lynne until she got a ride the driver would have known that there would be a witness if anything happened to her.

A2: With a witness nearby only a decent driver would stop.

A3: Let's assume the highly unlikely scenario that the first car by within a minute or two after Steven left Lynne all alone—just happened to be the one stranger who would want to harm her.

A4: This mysterious stranger who just happened by the intersection must also happen to be a pedophile.

A5: This stranger pedophile that just happened by must also happened to be in his raping, killing mood.

A6: After being with the little girl for several hours and not feeding her, this beat all-odds killer would reverse his direction and return to the very intersection where he picked up his victim.

A7: This pedophile without brains does not leave her out at the intersection. The hypothetical stranger takes more risk. He parks along a county road or turns left at a tractor trail and drives in the dark onto a 20-odd acre woodlot. There he stops his car, opens the door, gets out, and leads his victim to Steven's favorite spot in strange woods in the dark of night.

A8: He would bring poor Lynne back to the very area where people are looking for her and eyeing any strange movement.

A9: There he rapes and strangles Lynne with her own blouse. He picks up her panties as a souvenir but drops them 33 feet away instead of taking them to his car.

Questions and Answers about Truscott's Case

A10. You could never beat this for luck!? In the dark, this stranger would happen to pick the same bush area where Steven and Lynne were last seen together.

A11: **When friends tease Truscott, he makes up a story about looking for calves in the bush. When the police question him, he invents a car at the highway. When his penis sores are found his stories change with every telling.**

Q: Was Lynne raped?
A: While the attack clearly appears to be sexual, the forensic evidence does not *conclusively* **indicate penetration.**

Q: How could a 14-year old boy kill a 12-year old friend and then be calm and collected when he returned to his schoolmates?
A: His classmates said Steven was a tough, cool kid. Consider that anyone who can convince authorities and the public to reduce his sentence from hanging until dead to ten years and freedom, and later rally tax-payers to give him C$6.5 million for a crime he committed and found guilty is probably capable of killing a little 12 year old girl.
(Clue 114)

Q: Why did his peers find Truscott guilty of murdering Harper?

A1: This case would go to the jury with five witnesses saying that they did not see Steven and Lynne on the road to Highway 8 and two of them were actively looking for him.
When the jury found Truscott guilty of Lynne Harper's murder they may have been thinking this: Instead of taking Lynne to Highway 8 he left the county road and took her into the bush. That is what most witnesses have believed all along.

Questions and Answers about Truscott's Case

A2: The 1959 jury watched and listened carefully to 74 witnesses and was certain beyond any reasonable doubt that the overwhelming evidence in this mostly circumstantial case showed that Steven Truscott was the guilty person.

A3: The Jury was convinced that witnesses saw Steven and Lynne before reaching Lawson's Bush but no one saw them afterward. Rumors were flying around school that Steven was in the bush with Lynne even before her body was found.

Q: Why on Jan 20, 1960 did a five-judge Ontario Court unanimously dismiss Truscott's appeal?

A: They ruled the original trial was fair and in accordance with the law. *(2)*

Truscott said, *"This was the first news I received that a stay of execution had been ordered. I was dazed and it was some time before the full significance of what had occurred got through to me. I wasn't going to die!"* ***Perhaps there would be yet another miracle, an appeal, a new trial, even an acquittal."*** *(7, p.54)*

A: An innocent person would consider a stay of execution the right thing to do, not a miracle. An innocent person on death row prays that whoever killed the victim will be caught and confess to the murder. He would then be set free and exonerated; much better than getting a new trial and being acquitted. Yet Truscott doesn't speak of that. **It never crosses his mind or the minds of supporters that the best for him is for the killer to be found. For Truscott, this isn't an option because he knows that he is the only person responsible for Lynne's death.**

Steven Truscott: *"In August 1964, more than five years after my arrest, the Parole Board said I was eligible for parole and that I could apply for one on a form available through the classification department. I secured a form, filled it out, and in desperation to gain my freedom, I did something very stupid. In the space reserved for personal comments, I wrote that if I were released I would not be in trouble again."(7)* *(Clue 115)*

A: It is also possible that in his desperation to get out of prison he decided to write what he knew to be true.

Q: Why did Truscott's testimony before the Supreme Court contradict the testimony of nearly every other witness?

A: Truscott's story was that he took Lynne to the Highway 8 intersection. That was his story and he was sticking to it. So he denied or called incorrect the testimony of nearly every witness.

Steven Truscott says in his book: *One reporter referred to me as a 'cool customer', and another, as 'clever and devious.'... As to 'clever and devious', had I* **intended** *to rape and murder Lynne Harper, would I not, rather have been stupid beyond belief, to drive* **my** *victim, minutes prior to killing her, past innumerable witnesses? This fact occurred to no one, not even* **my** *counsel."* *7, p.49 (116)*

A: Certainly Steven **did not intend to kill Lynne, but** *Steven Truscott* **did confess indirectly to murdering Lynne Harper:** He does not state that he drove *her* or that he drove *the* victim. **He tells us that he drove** "**my victim.**" Pronouns give responsibility. By using the pronoun **"my"** he takes possession of the victim. **That was his counsel ("my counsel") and that was his victim ("my victim").** *12*

Judge: *What did the psychiatrists want from you?*
Truscott: *They wanted me to admit I killed Lynne.*
Judge: *What did you do?*
Truscott: *I would not admit it.* *(5)* Clue 117

Q: Why all the fuss? All the Truscott camp ever wanted was a new trial and acquittal.

A: **What the Truscott camp wanted was for Truscott to be found innocent and receive a lot of money.** Except for persecuting an innocent airman who, like Truscott, was never close to county road and Highway 8 on June 9th, you rarely hear the Truscott faithful talk about the "real killer being caught." *12*

Truscott said, *"I have paid five years of my life but this has taught me that crime does not pay, so all I ask is please grant me one chance to make a success of my life and prove that one dreadful mistake does not mean that I will ever make another."* **The above was taken from Truscott's 1964 parole application. Obviously he felt he had paid for his crime and wanted to do more with his life. If released he would stay crime-free and be productive**. *(Clue 118)*

Q: Why did the Canada Supreme Court rule 8-1 against a new trial for Truscott? *(Clue 119)*

A1. The Supreme Court watched and listened carefully to 21-year old Steven Truscott as he gave his testimony and it was clear to them that his testimony was confused and vague; and that some of his statements to the court were clearly inaccurate. *5*

A2: Truscott claimed not to remember and they felt he was lying. In some respects, far from assisting Truscott, his inaccuracies tended to contradict the defence position. *5*

Questions and Answers about Truscott's Case

Questions and Answers about Truscott's Case

A3: The Supreme Court of Canada stated that "There were incredibilities inherent in the evidence given by Truscott before us and we do not believe his testimony." Reference, re R. v. Truscott, supra, at p. 345. Supreme Court of Canada in their decision.

A4: The Court ruled 8-1 that it would have upheld conviction on the basis that the conduct of the provincial trial was fair and legal. *5*

A5: "The verdict of the jury, read in the light of the charge of the trial judge, makes it clear that they were satisfied beyond a reasonable doubt that the facts, established by the evidence which they accepted, were not only consistent with the guilt of Truscott but were inconsistent with any rational conclusion other than that Truscott was the guilty person. *5*

Q: Why was the public bombarded with media commentary supporting Truscott's claim of innocence?

A: Three main reasons are money for them; fame and sympathy for Steven Truscott.

Q: How could Truscott be guilty in this fully circumstantial case?

A: The case against Truscott was predominantly but not exclusively one of circumstantial evidence. *Judge Hall describing exactly the evidence against Steven Truscott:* "I recognize fully that guilt can be brought home to an accused by **circumstantial evidence**; that there are cases where the circumstances can be said to point inexorably to guilt more reliably than direct evidence. The circumstantial evidence case is built piece by piece until the final evidentiary structure completely entraps the prisoner in a situation from which he cannot escape." *J. Hall, dissenting judge. (5)*

Q: Why did Truscott blame his deplorable performance before the Supreme Court on lawyers: *"My lawyers did not prepare me adequately for my testimony before the Court of Appeal."*

A: Steven Truscott believes he can do no wrong; other people are always the ones at fault. *He believed he was smarter than professional people with their training and years of experience. Here we have the most notorious criminal case in Canadian history, an unprecedented hearing before the Supreme Court of Canada after an eight year public battle, the best criminal lawyers in the country, all this new expert evidence on human digestion that will exonerate wrongly convicted Steven Truscott.* **Yet no one on the crack defense team thinks to prepare their star client for his testimony?!** *(14)* **Regardless, how much preparation does Steven Truscott require to tell the truth, the whole truth, and nothing but the truth?** *(Clue 120)*

Q: What are some "incredibilities" that the Canada Supreme Court judges talk about?
A1): In 1966, new forensic evidence was presented on his behalf and 21-year old Truscott and 25 witnesses testified testified to the best of their abilities before Canada's Supreme Court where he told his story for the first time.
A2): Truscott was vague and confused and his testimony contradicted other witnesses. The Justices did not believe his testimony. *5*

A3): When Judges catch your testimony in lies, blame the lawyers for being found guilty of a crime you committed.

Q: Why did the Ontario Court of Appeal decide to review Truscott's conviction?

A1: Media blitz kept the Truscott story going, working the public into a frenzy thereby increasing sales and profits.

A2: Truscott mania supported by media sound bites and simple sympathetic statements instead of facts and logic.

Questions and Answers about Truscott's Case

Following is a quote from the Ontario Appeal Court Citation:
Truscott (Re), 2007 ONCA 575 Docket: C42726 Date: 20070828

*Concerning the third pillar of the Crown's case, in the County Road evidence, the **Ontario Court of Appeal Judges stated they are satisfied that Truscott could reasonably believe that he saw the color of the license plate on the vehicle while standing on the bridge** 1300 feet away.* 15

A2: If Steven Truscott, who was found to have normal eyesight, can see a license plate from 1300 feet then his friends can do likewise. Using 1300 feet set as a benchmark by the Court of Appeal Judges, we must assume that the seven or more kids on the straight, clear County Road would have seen a tall boy in red pants riding double with a girl on his distinctive green bicycle from 1300 feet away. In addition several kids, including Butch and Jocelyne, were actively looking for Steven. If Steven and Lynne were on County Road during the times given by Steven, seven witnesses would have seen them beyond Lawson's Bush. They were not seen because Steven had turned with Lynne into Lawson's Bush where her body would be found two days later.

Q: Why did the Canadian government find Truscott not guilty and compensate him with C$6.5 million of taxpayer's money?

A1: To satisfy the maddening crowd that was ready to riot if Truscott were found guilty.

A2: To appease some people that would rather be told what to think than to look themselves for facts and evidence.

A3: To increase media profits from a never ending crime story.

Q: Are Truscott supporters correct when they say the military was prepared to go to any lengths to shield one of its own?
A: The notion that the RCAF would frame a 14-year old boy in order to let a homicidal pedophile run free is frankly too absurd for comment. *13 (121)*

Q: Why wasn't pedophile Sgt. Kalichuk arrested since his brand new car matched Truscott's description.

A: It did not match. Truscott said he saw Lynne get into a **grey 1959 Chevrolet Bel Air** which he was able to recognize from the fins and the cats' eye shape tail lights. **Kalichuk's car was a 1959 canary yellow Pontiac Stratochief.** *(Clue 122)*

Q: Why wasn't the army man arrested for Lynne's murder?

A1: No evidence was found against Kalichuk or any other soldier so one was never arrested or charged.

A2: Kalichuk's sexual offenses consisted of indecent exposure and of trying to get young girls into his car. *42*

A3: There is no evidence that Kalichuk, like Truscott, was anywhere near the intersection on June 9, 1959. *(Clue 123)*

Q: Why are many crimes solved years later?

A1: The criminal is caught committing another crime.

A2: The criminal confesses because of guilt or remorse.

A3: While unbelievable to laymen, seasoned detectives catch criminals who could not stop bragging about their crime.

A4: In a high profile case such as this, the killer would feel a need to brag that he killed Lynne Harper and to show he is smarter than the police because he got away with murder.

A5: Fact: "loose lips" solve crimes years after they were thought unsolvable. The guilty confess their crime to a close friend or lover, or even to a stranger while drunk or depressed, who tells the police, out of fear, for revenge, reward, or sense of civic duty.

A6: Some guilty criminals who maintain their innocence from day one convince themselves that they are innocent. Some, like OJ Simpson, block the incident from memory and eventually believe their own unbelievable story and stick with it, no matter how ridiculous it may sound to others.

A7: No one in 50 years of this highly publicized crime has presented any evidence that someone other than Truscott killed Lynne and the passing of time makes it even more evident that Steven Truscott is the guilty person. *(Clue 124)*

Q: Why did the Canadian government give Steven Truscott C$6.5 million of taxpayer's money to compensate for the ten years spent in prison for killing Lynne Harper?
A: To appease those Canadians who prefer that the media tell them what and how to think.

The Harper family, usually forgotten by the media and Truscott advocates, is convinced of Truscott's guilt. The victim's older brother has publicly called the payment to Truscott a travesty, saying, **"Steven Truscott's quest to clear his name was motivated by money; the end game in this whole thing for Truscott was financial gain." A shameful hollow sham contrived to receive tax payer money for a crime Truscott himself committed.** News of the payout seriously affected the health of Lynne's aged father. It is shameful how this man has caused Canadian people to harm the Harper family. *(Clue 125)*

The evidence is that Steven Truscott didn't finish his sentence when he said, "I was in the wrong place at the wrong time"; he should have finished with "*and did the wrong thing.*"

Lynne Harper's Sacrifice

The real victim in this case is the energetic, delightful girl in the Harper family whose life ended at 12 years. She did not live 60 plus years as did most of her friends, including Steven.

She lost her life but may have saved other innocent girls from losing their lives. Perhaps while in prison Truscott learned to control his tough-boy tendencies. He was never charged with another crime; instead he set his goal to convince himself and others that he was not the killer. **A gullible public did him one better: gave him C$6.5 million for his crime. Then they gave his wife C$100,000. Calculating C$6,600,000/87,600 hours =over C$75 (seventy five dollars for every hour in prison.)**

Facts, Logic, and Critical Thinking

This is not just a story about a 14 year old schoolboy killing his 12 year old classmate. That case was settled when 12 jurors found the boy guilty and 13 Justices upheld the verdict over the next 48 years. The boy served 10 years for his crime, which seems justice deserved for a murder for young passion. *(Clue 126)*

This story is mainly about a money-hungry media and a gullible public who preferred sound bites and simple thoughts over the thoughtful analysis of jurors who listened to the testimony of 94 real witnesses. In addition, Canada's Supreme Court Justices questioned, watched, and listened to 26 witnesses give direct testimony under oath until they found the absolute truth.

The OPP remains steadfast that they performed well, had the right man, and made a solid case, without any doubt. No one there thinks he is innocent. Though every court that had full witness testimony found Truscott guilty and a liar, the media took Steven's "poor me" attitude and tried to make him into a saint. Many are still furious at what they see as biased reporting when ***The Fifth Estate's*** film made the OPP look as if they framed this kid.

Chapter 8: Second Truscott Victim RCAF Sergeant Alexander Kalichuk

Many followers of the Truscott biased media are convinced that police authorities looked only at Truscott and not at the several pedophiles living at RCAF stations. A favorite, whose picture is often linked to the murder of Lynne Harper, is RCAF **Sergeant Alexander Kalichuk.**

To free Steven Truscott's name from the murder of Lynne Harper, *The Fifth Estate* presented a different suspect's name, RCAF Sergeant Alexander Kalichuk who was safely dead and therefore not a libel threat. An investigation by *The Fifth Estate*, assisted by the National Archives in Ottawa, retrieved the 900-page dossier on Kalichuk. It indicated that he was a heavy drinker and a troubled man with arrests for sexual offenses. Canadian Journalists uncovered military files that found the 35-year old had worked on an air base an hour away, sometimes visited Clinton, and who sold a car shortly after Lynne's murder.

Alexander Kalichuk served in the Royal Canadian Air Force during World War II. Honorably discharged in 1945, the Airman returned to civilian life and in 1950 he re-enrolled in the RCAF.

Sgt. Kalichuk's Criminal Record: *In 1950 a Trenton Court fined Sgt. Kalichuk $10 for two convictions of indecent exposure.* Twelve days before Lynne's murder, Sgt. Kalichuk spotted three young farm girls on a country road near St. Thomas, Ontario. He tried to lure a 10-year old into his car by offering her a new pair of panties. He left when he saw the girl's father approaching. Kalichuk was later arrested but the charges were dismissed for lack of evidence but he gave Kalichuk a warning regarding his behavior. No evidence he ever got a girl in his car.

Steven Truscott did not see Sgt. Kalichuk's car. Truscott has maintained that he saw Lynne get into a grey Chevrolet Bel Air that he recognized by the fins and cats' eye shape to the tail lights, from 1300 feet away. Kalichuk sold his car three weeks after Lynne's murder. All that fuss over the car fizzled out once it was known that the vehicle he sold was a canary yellow Pontiac, not a grey Chevrolet. *(Clue 127)*

In the wake of Truscott supporter disappointments, came the inevitable accusations of a military cover-up. According to conspiracists, the military was prepared to go to any length to shield one of its own. The notion that the RCAF would frame a 14-year-old schoolboy in order to let a homicidal pedophile run free is frankly **too absurd for comment**.

Whereas there is no evidence that Sgt. Kalichuk was even in Clinton at the time of Lynne Harper's death, **Truscott's presence on County Road that hot June evening is a matter of record**. Sgt Kalichuk died in 1975 in a psychiatric hospital in Goderich, Ontario, possibly from alcoholism.

Conclusion

It is common ground that if Steven Truscott crossed the bridge and dropped Lynne Harper off at Highway 8, then he is innocent. **On the other hand, if Steven did not take Lynne to Highway 8, but instead took her into the bush where her body was later found, then it is a virtual certainty that he killed her.**

It is common ground that if a passerby on busy Highway 8 saw a boy or girl, a boy and girl, or a bicycle at the intersection between 7:30 and 7:45 pm on June 9, 1959, then Truscott is innocent. **On the other hand, if absolutely no one said they saw a boy or girl near the intersection around the time Truscott said he was there, then he did not reach the highway with Lynne but instead took her into Lawson's Bush and it is a virtual certainty that Steven killed Lynne. Even with the case a national obsession no one, none, not even one person came forward with any such sighting.**

People who have not thought clearly and objectively about this case imagine their own bogeyman, an Army "pedophile", rather than examine **Truscott's own unusual and suspicious actions:**

(1) That **one hour before dark**, Steven said Lynne asked him to take her 1.2 miles to Highway 8 so she could see ponies nearby;

(2) That **Steven took her on his crossbar with his arms around her** and let her off with no talk about how she would get to the farm house nearby, or how she would get home before dark;

(3) That Steven **Truscott left Lynne standing alone at the intersection** instead of waiting to see if she would be safe;

(4) That Truscott turned around and rode slowly back to the bridge and when **he looked back 1300 feet towards the intersection he said he saw Lynne's arm out hitch-hiking and watched as she got into a stranger's 1959 Chevrolet Bel Air and speed east down fairly busy King's Highway 8;**

(5) That **after seeing his girl friend sped away by a stranger Truscott turned to watch and wave to his friends in the river, saying nothing** to them about the tragic event he had just witnessed;

(6) That after several minutes of watching and waving, Steven rides off to meet with school mates, **again saying nothing about Lynne's ride with a stranger** until classmate Warren Hatherall, who had seen Truscott returning to the school without Lynne, asked, *"What happened to Harper; did you feed her to the fish?" Truscott said he replied, "No, I just let her off at the highway." There is no evidence of any other remark.* (15, p. 322);

(7) That **Truscott did not bother to go to the Harper home** and tell them that he had just left Lynne alone on Highway 8.

(8) That **Truscott did not bother to tell Mr. Harper** the next morning that yesterday he witnessed his daughter hitch-hiking and get into the front seat with a strange man heading east;

(9) This is where Truscott supporters take over the unbelievable imaginary tale and **make the "stranger who picked Lynne up" into a military pedophile who drives away from the station with Lynne** for a few hours or a day, without feeding her;

(10) That the boogeyman military pedophile decides to take Lynne back, not to the intersection where he picked her up, but to **leave her body in Truscott's favorite place in Lawson's Bush;**

(11) Never mind that searchers are checking every movement in and around Lawson's Bush because **this "invisible killer" is unseen and is able to leave not a trace that he was there.**

Consider that among the overwhelming evidence presented in 1959 was that *Truscott's classmates teased him about being in the bush with Lynne* before her body was found.

Consider that **the legal system** that **unanimously found Steven guilty in 1959 consisted of his peers who heard witnesses directly involved in the incident. And those jurors were not under duress while making their decision.**

Consider that in 1966-7, new forensic evidence was presented on his behalf and **21-year old Steven Truscott** testified before the Supreme Court judges who said he was vague and confused and could not remember any details. His statements were in conflict with the testimony of the 23 reliable witnesses.

Nine Judges asked questions, watched and listened carefully to all the witnesses as they gave testimony, and it was clear to them that Truscott's testimony was vague and confused---and they did not believe him. Canada's top judges ruled 8-1 against Truscott's appeal and sent him back to prison to serve the remainder of his life sentence.

To be fair Truscott, believing he can do no wrong, claimed his defense lawyers, some of Canada's finest, did not "adequately prepare" him for testifying before the Supreme Court. **How much time and effort is required to be prepared to tell the truth, the whole truth, and nothing but the truth?**

Consider that **the legal system that acquitted Truscott in 2007 made its decision 48 years after the crime was committed, and that their opinion was very likely driven by Truscott mania prevalent throughout Canada**. *(11)*

Defense asked the court for a declaration of innocence. After their "under duress" decision, *the Ontario Appeal Court was still of the view that* **Mr. Truscott had not demonstrated his factual innocence.** "…certain immutable facts casting suspicion on Mr. Truscott – in particular: that *Steven was the last person known to have seen Lynne alive, and the fact that Steven was with Lynne close to the location where she was murdered* – made demonstrating his innocence particularly difficult."*(15)*

Consider that the lesson of Steven Truscott is that **a media blitz and public emotions in place of facts, logic, and critical thinking can be a constant peril to any justice system.** There is nothing like a good murder to increase media profits, especially when a young boy had been sentenced to death.

Critical thinking people know that the facts presented in this case **go well beyond preponderance of the evidence. They comprise moral certainty that Steven killed Lynne Harper.**

There is an unconscious desire on the part of many to find greater meaning in the life and trials of Steven Truscott than is possible based on the historical case. **And so for them, there will always be an innocent Truscott. It simply has to be.**

Any way…that's how I see it. Feel free to disagree.

Dear Reader,

Hi, my name is **Sam Dennis** McDonough. I have attempted to compile and present facts and evidence that lead to the truth in Canada's most infamous crime, the murder of Lynne Harper.

I first heard about the Truscott-Harper crime in August, 2010 when it was shown on Discovery ID. This was a simple crime and easy to see who was guilty. I was unaware that so many people had such passionate feelings about this murder until I posted on the internet. It seems that about 90% of Canadians **believe** Truscott did not kill Lynne Harper while the 10% of critical thinking Canadians, including the Ontario Appeal judges, are **certain** he is **not innocent** of the crime.

No matter if you think Steven Truscott is guilty or not, my hope is that you got some insight toward the truth in this crime. Like everyone, I hate to see the innocent go to prison and I do not like to see the guilty free to kill again. But even more, **I really hate to see a killer get well paid for his crime.**

SDM

sammcdon@gmail.com

Truth will always be truth...regardless of lack of understanding, disbelief or ignorance. W. Clement Stone

Readers who found these facts and evidence interesting or fascinating can find other books about controversial true crimes that are essential reading for true-crime enthusiasts.

120 Clues that Show Who Killed **Jon Benet** (Ramsey) ;
Go to Sleep Baby, Mommy has to PARTY (**Caylee Anthony**) ;
Oswald, Conspirators, John F. Kennedy (**JFK assassination**)
The West Memphis Boogieman (the **WM3 murderers**) ;
O. J. Simpson Murders, Who killed Nicole Brown and Ron Goldman and Why the jury found O. J. Simpson Not Guilty

Until someone can Explain...

Until someone can explain why **Steven Truscott supporters ignore the fact that** in 1966-7, *the Canada Supreme Court found 22-year-old Steven Truscott's testimony before them vague and confused and didn't believe a word he said.*

Until **Truscott explains why he asked a girl into the woods** *to see calves rather than a boy or best friend Butch George?*

Until someone can explain why **Steven Truscott proposed a secret date with Jocelyne Goddette** to see calves in the woods and *told her not to tell anybody and not to bring anyone*?

Until someone can explain **why Jocelyne would be looking for Steven Truscott** on the right hand side of the county road *if he had not previously told her to meet him there?*

Until someone explains why the *Fifth Estate's* **biased movie** showed Lynne on the *handle bars* instead of the crossbar as was testified by Steven Truscott and every witness who saw them?

Until someone can explain why **they believe Truscott's story of hitch-hiking** when there is *absolutely no evidence that Lynne was planning to leave her home and her parents and head east with the first stranger who picked her up.*

Until someone can explain why anyone would believe Truscott's story that Lynne wanted to go 1.2 miles to the highway to **hitch-hike alone at 7:30 when she had to be home by 8:30 pm.**

Until someone can give evidence that this child ever had shown the **disposition or desire to run away from home.**

Until someone explains **why they accept Steven's story that Lynne wanted a ride to the highway** to see ponies and when she got there *decided instead to hitch-hike to who knows where?*

Until supporters explain why they believe a decent boy would take a petite 12-year-old girl friend on his bicycle cross-bar and **then leave her alone at an isolated spot one hour before dark.**

Until someone can explain the above ten evidences of guilt, I will have full confidence that Steven Truscott murdered petite Lynne Harper in Lawson's Bush.

Until someone can explain why Truscott, after seeing the girl friend he had just left alone suddenly get into a stranger's car, he did not mention this tragic event to his friends at the bridge. If this story **actually happened, even Truscott would have the maturity and decency** *to tell his friends that she may be in danger; at least a mention to his friend Douglas Oats.*

Until someone can explain why they accept Truscott's kindness for taking Lynne to the highway, *but forgive him for leaving his friend alone.* Steven has always said that he took her there, let her off, and rode back to the bridge, without conversation.

Until someone can explain why generous good-hearted Truscott, after taking Lynne 1.2 miles to the highway, **would not offer to take her .3 miles further to the pony farm or at least stay with her until she was safe from the danger of being left all alone.**

Until someone can explain why *Truscott did* not *school chums or his brother* that he had given Lynne Harper a ride to the intersection where he saw her get into a stranger's 1959 Chevy Bel Air and speed away and that her life is in danger. *If the story were true, Steven would have told them what he claimed he saw after he was asked if he threw Lynne Harper to the fish.* **Saying nothing about his tragic event story is proof positive of guilt.**

Until Steven Truscott can tell us why he **did not notify anyone** *that he saw his girl friend hitch a ride with a stranger*

Until someone can explain the above five evidences of guilt, I will have full confidence that Steven Truscott murdered Lynne Harper in Lawson's Bush.

Until Steven Truscott explains why he did not tell us in his book that he dropped Lynne Harper off at the Highway 8 intersection? He may have dropped Lynne off, but the evidence is that he did not drop her off at the highway because *her body was found in the bush near where she was last seen with him.*

Until someone can explain why, after a sleepless grief-stricken night, Lynne's **father had to go to Steven Truscott at his home to find out what he did with his 12-year-od daughter.**

Until Steven Truscott tells us why he told Mr. Harper only that Lynne *wanted a ride to see some ponies and that he rode her to the Highway 8 where he left her unharmed*.

Until **Steven Truscott tells us why he did not say to the concerned father** that he was *sorry he had left his 12-year-old daughter alone at the intersection one hour before dark.*

Until **Steven Truscott tells us why** he did not tell the worried father his favorite story *that he saw her hitch-hiking to who knows where.* He saves that story for his first police interview.

Until someone can explain the above five evidences of guilt, I will have full confidence that Steven Truscott murdered Lynne Harper in Lawson's Bush.

Until Truscott tells us why he did not tell the grieving father that *he saw Lynne get into a stranger's 1959 Chevrolet Bel Air and that he saw the car speeding east down highway 8.*

Until Truscott tells why *he would tell his unbelievable story to the police that morning, but not earlier to the grieving father?*

Until someone can explain why anyone would *believe the made up unbelievable story that the only car to stop for Lynne* would happen to be *a stranger who would harm her?*

Until someone can explain why Truscott supporters believe, without question, his wild unbelievable story **that a mysterious stranger picked Lynne up on the highway,** rode around with her for hours without feeding her, would reverse his direction *and return her, mind you, not to the intersection where he picked her up, but to kill her in Truscott's favorite place in a dark 20 acre bush;* all without leaving one piece of evidence that he was there.

Until someone can explain how it could *happen that a driver or passenger on this fairly busy highway did not report seeing a girl, or boy, or girl and boy, or a distinct green racer bike* during the 10 or so minutes that Steven Truscott says they were there.

Until someone can explain the above five evidences of guilt, I will have full confidence that Steven Truscott murdered Lynne Harper in Lawson's Bush.

Until someone can explain *why Truscott's supporters believe, against all odds, that the mysterious stranger to happen by would also happen to be a pedophile, and in the killing mood.*

Until someone explains how *this brainless pedophile, in the dark, would happen to pick the same woodlot that Truscott said he and Lynne rode by just a few hours earlier.*

Until Truscott tells us that he *really did tell the truth to three different police officers that he and Richard Gellanty passed each other* before reaching the bush and that he later lied under oath that he did not see Gellanty, and that he testified falsely that he never told any police officer that he saw or passed Gellanty.

Until someone can explain why Steven Truscott ever felt he had to say, "I was in the woods chasing a cow", if *he had actually taken Lynne straight to the intersection.*

Until Steven Truscott tells us why it was that when friends teased him about being in the woods with Lynne, *he told them a story about looking for calves in the bush.* When police questioned him, *he invented a new Chevrolet Bel Air with yellow license plates that he could see from 1300 feet.* And when his penis sores were found *his stories changed with every telling, until 48 years later he said there never were any sores.*

Until Steven Truscott has a *believable reason why he had two raw lesions* the size of quarters on either side of his penis shaft just days after Lynne's attempted rape and murder?

Until someone can explain the above six evidences of guilt, I will have full confidence that Steven Truscott murdered Lynne Harper in Lawson's Bush.

Until someone can explain why *Truscott supporters do not believe the testimony of the many people who witnessed the actual events and who knew the most truth about this case. They testified in court under oath, something Steven Truscott did only one time and failed miserably.*

Until someone explains why Truscott supporters will not accept the finding of the original Ontario Appeal Court in 1960 that Steven *Truscott's trial was fair and in accordance with law*.

Until someone explains why *Truscott's testimony under oath before the Supreme Court of Canada contradicted the testimony of every other witness?* (Except that of his three family friends)

Until someone can explain why *Steven Truscott supporters ignore the fact that in 1966-7, the Canada Supreme Court found* **22-year-old Steven Truscott's testimony before them vague and confused** *and didn't believe a word he said.*

Until someone can explain why Truscott supporters ignore the judgment of the 1967 Canada Supreme Court whose Justices made it clear that they were "*satisfied beyond a reasonable doubt that the facts*, which they found established by evidence which they accepted, *were not only consistent with the guilt of Truscott but were inconsistent with any rational conclusion other than that* Steven Truscott was the guilty person.*"*

Until someone can explain why in the wake of defeat at the Supreme Court, **Truscott supporters tried to dig up evidence to support his story.** The Steven Truscott Defense Committee placed full-page ads in the *Huron Expositor* appealing to eyewitnesses to come forward. The ad read, "**If anyone saw Lynne Harper that evening Truscott can still be proved innocent!**" The **Result: Not one person saw Lynne Harper**.

Until someone can explain why, "the Ontario Court of Appeal judges were **satisfied that Truscott could reasonably believe that he saw the color of the license plate on the vehicle from 1300 feet away**" *but did not consider in their timeline* that his schoolmates should also see Steven and Lynne riding double on his distinctive green bike from less than 100 feet away.

Until someone can explain why supporters accept every *false sound bite* about Sgt. Kalichuk as true, but will not consider f*acts and evidence that prove he could not be Lynne's killer.* The 900 page file retrieved by the *Fifth Estate* has not even a hint of involvement by Kalichuk in the death of Harper or of any violence toward anyone, male or female. He was arrested only once and that for indecent exposure. He attempted to get girls into his car but there is no evidence he ever succeeded. Truscott maintains that he saw Lynne get into a grey 1959 Chevy. Kalichuk owned a 1952 yellow Ford. Truscott believers chose to ruin Kalichuk and his family's reputation because he is deceased, not because he is guilty of a major crime. Shame on them!

Until someone can explain **each of the above evidences of guilt,** *I have full confidence that Steven Truscott murdered Lynne Harper in Lawson's Bush on June 9, 1959.* **And that he then spent the rest of his life fooling with the Canadian people.**

This Space Reserved

If you have evidence, physical or circumstantial, that anyone other than Steven Truscott murdered Lynne Harper enter the name here: _____

Nothing gives rest but the sincere search for truth. Blaise Pascal

Sources

1. **Magistrate's Court Preliminary Hearing**: *"Transcript of evidence heard at Goderich on July 13th-14th. 1959"*, His Worship Magistrate D. E. Holmes presiding.

2. **Court of Appeal for Ontario**, *Volume 5, The Appellant's Compendium*, January 20, 1960.

3. **LeBourdais, Isabel.** The Trial of Steven Truscott, Toronto: MClelland & Stewart, 1966.

4. *Toronto Daily Star* (October 6, 1966) and (October 13, 1966)

5. **Judgments of the Supreme Court of Canada** *Re: Steven Murray Truscott,* [1967] S.C.R. 309 Date: 1967-05-04

6. **Canada National Parole Board,** File C-K-6730, Oct. 22, 1968.

7. Who Killed Lynne Harper? *The Steven Truscott Story*, Pocket Book, 166 pages, **by Steven Truscott as told to Bill Trent.** 1971

8. **Jackson, Robert,** Steven Truscott *(Francis Camps* (London: Hart-Davis MacGibbon, 1975) p.28

9. **Simpson, Keith.** Professor. Forty Years of Murder: *An Autobiography.* London: George G. Harrap, 1978

10. Until you are Dead, *"Steven Truscott's Long Ride into History"* by **Julian Sher** [2000]

11. *The Fifth Estate* (March 29, 2000)

12. Statement Analysis *by* **Mark McClish** *of the* Steven Truscott Story by Steven Truscott *as told to Bill Trent,* Pocket Book edition, 166 pages. Remarks posted July 9, 2001

13. A Question of Evidence **by Colin Evans**, Chapter 9 [2003] Steven Truscott A Time for Dying

14. A Few Thoughts about an Innocent Man, **Robert Collings**, My reflections on reading Julian Sher's *Until You Are Dead*, 2004

15. **Court of Appeal for Ontario,** Citation: Truscott (Re), 2007 ONCA 575 Docket: C42726 Date: 20070828

16. Victim's family stunned by Truscott compensation. CBC News 7/8/2008

17. Ontario Ministry of the Attorney General; Entitlement to Compensation - The Legal Framework; *attorneygeneral.jus.gov.on.ca/english*

Printed in Great Britain
by Amazon